"By the powers of earth, fire, wind and sea, I command thee: unmask!"

She felt a surge of power in the arm she held. And then the woman's body shimmered—there was no other word for it—and resolved itself into…

A man.

And an amazingly handsome man, at that. Tall—very tall—broad shouldered under a leather jacket, much bigger than she was, powerful through the chest and thighs. Longish hair curled around his ears, and he was wearing jeans worn so soft they looked like buckskin, all of which gave him a roguish, buccaneering look.

"Well done," he commented, looking infuriatingly pleased with her.

"What are you playing at, shifter?" Cait demanded, while simultaneously scanning the room behind him for a weapon. Being located down a mysterious, romantic alley was a big plus for atmosphere. It was not such an ideal situation when you found yourself suddenly alone with a rogue shapeshifter.

"I'm not playing, Keeper. I'm not playing at all."

ALEXANDRA SOKOLOFF

is a California native and the daughter of scientist and educator parents, which drove her into musical theater at an early age.

At U.C. Berkeley (a paranormal experience all on its own) she majored in theater; wrote, directed and acted in all sorts of productions from Shakespeare to street theater; trained in modern dance; directed and choreographed four full-scale musicals; spent a summer singing in a Montana bar; and graduated Phi Beta Kappa.

After college Alex moved to Los Angeles, where she has made an interesting living writing novel adaptations, and original suspense and horror scripts for numerous Hollywood studios.

The Harrowing, her debut ghost story, was nominated for both a Bram Stoker Award (horror) and an Anthony Award (mystery) as Best First Novel. The book is based on a real poltergeist experience from her high school years. She is the author of the paranormal mystery/thrillers *The Price, The Unseen* and *Book of Shadows,* and is the winner of a Thriller Award for her story *"The Edge of Seventeen."*

Alex is also the author of *Screenwriting Tricks For Authors,* a workbook based on her internationally acclaimed blog and writing workshops.

ALEXANDRA SOKOLOFF

THE SHIFTERS

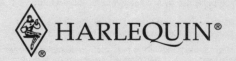

TORONTO • NEW YORK • LONDON
AMSTERDAM • PARIS • SYDNEY • HAMBURG
STOCKHOLM • ATHENS • TOKYO • MILAN • MADRID
PRAGUE • WARSAW • BUDAPEST • AUCKLAND

Recycling programs
for this product may
not exist in your area.

ISBN-13: 978-0-373-61846-0

THE SHIFTERS

Dear Reader,

I'm very excited to introduce my, well, my sixth book, actually, but my first-ever Harlequin Nocturne. I was thrilled when the lovely and stupendously talented Heather Graham asked me to cowrite a trilogy set in New Orleans, that fabulous like-no-other city where I've shared such fantastic times with Heather and our third cowriter, Deborah LeBlanc. Our mutual love of New Orleans and shared fascination with all things paranormal—and criminal—made brainstorming the series a dream: we got to use all our favorite places and what-ifs, and even some spooky experiences (the New Orleans cemeteries at night, the vampire and ghost walks, a séance at a magic shop, the sense of the city at three in the morning).

I've written ghosts, witches, poltergeists and even a character who may just be the devil, but this book was my first time out with vampires, werewolves and shapeshifters. There is so much history in New Orleans, it was a lark to create a species of beings who had been around for some of the…stranger stuff, and who live on the fringes of the fringe of this very fringe-y city. And it was no huge stretch to write about three powerful sisters when I was working with such powerful sisters in writing.

And I have to admit, I had a lot of fun with the sex. Scenes, I mean.

I hope you enjoy reading *The Shifters* as much as I did writing it.

Alexandra Sokoloff

For Heather Graham and all the Pozzessere clan, who have made New Orleans (and so many other places!) a true and beloved home away from home.

Chapter 1

The wind breathes over the Mississippi River, rippling the water, caressing the crescent of the New Orleans shore. It slips through the black iron gates of Jackson Square, stirring the colorful paintings by local artists carefully hung on the bars, and sweeps through the cobblestone Quarter, an old lover, knowing, familiar.

But this morning something rides the wind, something not gentle at all, knowing, but insidious, invisible and malevolent. The white cats sleeping on the shop steps shrink away from it, fur bristling in their slumber, and the magnolia trees shiver at its touch.

Evil.

* * *

Caitlin MacDonald shuddered awake in the pre-dawn, her heart racing.

Far above her a ceiling fan thrummed, and the stir of air on her flesh made her shiver again as the remnants of her dream rustled in her head insubstantially, like leaves in the wind.

Bad wind, she thought. *Something bad.*

She sat up in bed, pushing away a silky comforter, and reaching for a silver and black kimono that went with her riot of blond hair and silvery eyes.

The feeling of unease was worse as she stood, and her first jolted thoughts were of her sisters.

Fiona. Shauna. Are they all right?

She crossed her bedroom quickly, bare feet slipping across the gleaming old oak floors, and pulled open the French doors to step out onto the balcony.

In the soft humidity of the morning, she looked out over the compound, the enclosed stone-paved garden sheltered by the house, built in three wings around the square. Caitlin's every sense was on alert. The wind was strong, insistent, rustling the magnolia leaves and rippling through the hibiscus vines, splashing water from the center fountain onto the mossy paving stones. She froze as she glimpsed movement beside the brick wall, with its concealed gate out to the city street.

A sleek figure in black…sweatshirt hood shadowing its face…

The figure put its foot up on the rim of the fountain and bent over a leg, stretching. The hood dropped back, revealing a reddish-blond ponytail.

Caitlin slowly relaxed, recognizing her younger sister Shauna, warming up for her morning run. Caitlin leaned over the balcony railing, and Shauna, with her ever-present animal awareness, looked sharply up. Caitlin waved, and Shauna tossed her ponytail back. "Be careful!" Caitlin called down.

Shauna grinned and flipped a hand, dismissing the warning. Then she yanked open the gate, breaking into a run as soon as she'd shut and locked the iron door.

Caitlin breathed out, irked at Shauna's nonchalance, but somewhat reassured at such a normal reaction. Then a pale shape leapt into her peripheral vision, and she started back in shock….

Fur brushed against her hand, and Caitlin shook her head at her own jumpiness. "Chloe! You scared me," she scolded, reaching out to stroke the cat parading in front of her on the railing of the balcony—one of the cream and gold cats that roamed the compound, sisters upon sisters, as possessive of their space as if they'd been the ones who'd lived there for five generations. Which indeed they had, just as had the human MacDonald sisters.

Caitlin picked up the cat and cuddled it to her chest as she felt the wind stir again below them, saw the invisible force gather the branches of the trees into a swirling mass. She frowned again.

Fiona.

Caitlin looked across the garden to the wing of the house directly across from her own, her elder sister's apartments. The balcony was unmistakably Fiona's, overflowing with flowers, which seemed to burst into life when Fiona simply looked at them. The French doors were open a tad, and the sight made Caitlin's heart start beating faster again.

What if someone got in? What if I'm too late? What if this time she really does die because of me?

The wind billowed the filmy curtains that hung behind the French doors, and Caitlin's heart wrenched in sick anxiety.

Then the curtains were brushed aside and Fiona herself stepped out, oversize coffee cup in hand. Caitlin breathed a massive sigh of relief. Fiona stood at the railing for a moment, slender, gorgeous...the sunlight turning her long pure blond hair luminous as she looked out on the garden and then spotted Caitlin. Her lovely smile widened, and she raised her coffee cup.

Then the curtains moved behind her, and out

stepped a tall, superbly muscled, dark-haired man, wearing tight jeans and nothing else.

He didn't see Caitlin; his eyes were only on Fiona as he drew her into a kiss, openmouthed, hungry, and Caitlin watched in turmoil as her sister melted against him. The man raised his head and pulled Fiona back through the French doors with obvious intent.

Caitlin backed up and slipped through her own French doors, her heart pounding again, but this time in anger.

Damned vampire. How could Fiona be such a fool? Thinking she's in love with that—that Other.

Caitlin slammed the French doors behind her. All kinds of bad omens this morning. She didn't like it. Not at all.

Now dressed in a purple, green and gold peasant dress and comfortable beaded sandals—the Quarter's cobblestone sidewalks were hell on a girl's shoes—Caitlin moved out through the gate of the compound and into the soft light of day. She felt her unease begin to slip away.

She loved the Vieux Carre, the "old street," in the morning. New Orleans was a city of night owls, so Caitlin had the Quarter practically to herself in the early hours. Her daily ritual was to walk down to Café Du Monde, the famous coffee-and-beignets shop, for a tall cup of the smoothest, most fragrant, chicory-laced coffee on the planet, and then out to the Riverwalk to check on her city, test its perimeters, feel for any trouble.

She breathed in as she passed the shops with their treasures behind sparkling plate glass: the gilded clocks, antique mirrors and elegant furniture from another time, the intricate jewelry and the splashy colorful paintings, the enticing clothing; and the smells—fish and sweet liquor and sugar candles, Cajun cooking and coffee….

There was hardly a thing that was normal or modern about it, Caitlin mused as she turned down Pirates' Alley, walking past rustic storefronts on one side, the high iron bars that surrounded the gardens of St. Louis Cathedral on the other. New Orleans was a city out of time, existing in its own parallel universe.

And that made it a perfect settlement for Others.

For centuries, the Wild West, anything-goes atmosphere of New Orleans had made the city a natural draw for supernatural beings. Besides New Orleans' more famous contingent of ghosts and voodoo practitioners, there also existed secret societies of Others: vampires, werewolves and shape-shifters, who had migrated from all over the world to make their home here, living totally under the radar.

The migration had started in the late 1600s and early 1700s, when the new American colonies became an attractive means of escape for Others fleeing the ongoing witch persecutions in Europe. Official church doctrine had made it clear that all shapeshifters, werewolves, vampires and otherworldly beings were to be classified as witches, and subject to the same laws of torture and execution.

So the New World meant a new start for thousands of Others. And as America expanded Westward, and new cities sprang up with their own distinct characters, the Others naturally gravitated toward the unique port city of New Orleans, where French law was lax, the supernatural—in the form of voodoo— was an underlying thread of the culture, and open-mindedness and indulgence were a cherished part of daily life.

Where better to hide in plain sight than in a city where masks and costumes were the rule rather than the exception, where eccentricity not only thrived but was expected, and the constant influx of tourists made change a constant and too many questions about anyone's past…well, just plain rude.

It had been so for hundreds of years. And for hundreds of years the MacDonald clan had served as Keepers of the city, Keepers of the balance between the human and supernatural worlds. While the Others were perfectly aware of their human counterparts, and some lived fairly integrated lives, holding down human jobs and even owning businesses, few humans

knew just how many Others there were—if they had
any conception of the Others at all. It was how the
Others wanted it; every sane Other was mortally
aware of humankind's propensity to hunt down and
kill all that it did not understand. Not exactly witches,
but far more than ordinarily human, it was the Keepers who made sure, to the best of their abilities, that
didn't happen. It was also their job to make sure that
any supernatural shenanigans that encroached on
human life were handled with utmost discretion,
without exposing the existence of the communities.
Fiona served as the liaison with the vampires, Caitlin,
the shapeshifters, and Shauna, the were-packs. Each
sister was marked from birth with the sign of the beings she Kept, and each had developed certain skills
to help her manage her special charges. Since their
parents' untimely deaths, the three sisters had been
in sole charge of Keeping the city.

So it was in her official capacity as a Keeper
that Caitlin brooded that morning, brooded as she
walked the narrow street, with its closed shop fronts
and unique wood-shuttered windows set flush to the
sidewalk. Relieved though she was that her sisters
were fine, she was still keyed-up from her dream.
Caitlin's dreams were often precognitive, or at least
hypersensitive. This one had felt like more than a
dream; it had felt like danger. And she couldn't afford
to screw up again. She had been asleep at the wheel

the last time the city had been threatened by a rogue Other, but being in a fog of her own concoction was no excuse.

And her inattention had put Fiona in danger, had nearly killed her. Had nearly killed both of them.

It had been just three months since a series of homicides apparently committed by a rogue vampire had threatened the city, and Fiona, along with homicide detective and vampire Jagger DeFarge, had taken on the brunt of the investigation, the vampire community being Fiona's special purview.

It turned out the killer hadn't been a vampire at all, but a shapeshifter, who had taken on vampire abilities after years of concentrated shifting into vampire form. A pair of such shifters, actually. And shapeshifters were Caitlin's responsibility. Only she had been so—distracted...

She shut her mind down then.

No. I'm not going to think about it. It's never going to happen again.

But even as she thought it, she felt the touch of the wind brushing against her bare legs, slipping through her clothes....

The wind.

Her heart contracted again.

The wind...soft and enticing, the warm breath of the Quarter.

But something was off this morning, like the

dream. The wind was not comforting and caressing, that familiar invisible lover. Today there was an edge to it.

Bad wind, Caitlin thought again.

She stopped in front of the paintings hanging on the bars of the fencing around Jackson Square, looking around her. As her eyes swept over them, she recognized paintings from her dream.

And suddenly she had the distinct and unnerving sensation that she was being watched.

From the comfortable invisibility of the alley, he watched the Keeper.

She had been walking for blocks with no awareness of him. A bad sign—for her, anyway. For her—and for the city.

She was lovely, though, that rippling hair, blonde as moonlight, that ripe body, all that coiled strength and sweetness, pale and voluptuous curves. He felt it stir him, the thought of how it would feel to be inside that lusciousness....

Caitlin felt an intent, as clear as touch on her skin. She whirled and stared across the square at the intersection of streets.

There. A shadow, slipping quickly into Pirates' Alley.

She froze on the cobblestone walkway, her heart in her throat....

Then, without thinking, she ran back toward the alley.

He hovered in the alley, aware of her *sudden awareness, aroused by it.*

Unmask now?

Too easy. There was a time, and he would wait for it.

The Keeper whirled toward him and broke into a run, straight for the alley.

He slipped back, insubstantial as shadow.

Caitlin put on a burst of speed and tore around the corner of the Absinthe Bar, into the narrow alley.

There was no one. The flat stones of the street were empty. She whirled from side to side, staring, her breath coming harsh in her throat as she scanned the doorways of the closed shops. The wind whispered in the corners, swung the antique shop signs on their chains….

No one…but a feeling of presence and intent. Overwhelming, ominous. Gooseflesh rose on Caitlin's arm, crawled up her nape….

She backed away and ran.

Chapter 2

Armed with the largest café au lait available from Café Du Monde, Caitlin unlocked the door of A Little Bit of Magic, the mystic shop she and her sisters ran. Inside she locked the door firmly behind her; then, without even opening the wooden shutters of the bay windows, she marched back through the store, past the small coffee and tea bar, and the shelves of herbs and roots in glass jars, past bookcases of divinatory classics, histories of religion and magic traditions past and present, past jewelry cases full of sparkling gemstones set into intricate silver pieces and magical wands, to the doorway hung with its purple velvet curtain embroidered with glittering gold stars. She brushed through the soft folds into the reading room, a circular windowless space redolent with incense and hung with esoteric tapestries, a round table placed in the center, along with two high-backed chairs set across from each other.

Caitlin crossed to a wooden cupboard with painted symbols, and opened the doors to remove a silk-wrapped rectangle, her Tarot deck.

She breathed in, possibly for the first time since she'd entered the shop, and forced herself to be still, to focus, to release tension, to breathe from her center. When she had quieted her pulse, she stepped more deliberately to a hanging wooden shelf and took a match, which she struck to light the candles on the table, and then the ones in the tall metal candelabrum in the corner.

After that she sat in one of the chairs, facing the back wall, centered the deck before her and un-wrapped it. She closed her eyes and mixed the cards, once, twice, three times, spoke aloud the name of the city itself as querent, and laid out a simple spread: Past, Present, Future.

"Where have you been?" she asked aloud, then reached and turned over a card.

The Tower. Destruction. That was Katrina, of course, still a wound, leaving the city vulnerable. It also had overtones of the war between the Other races that had killed her parents, and of the recent upheaval in the communities because of the cemetery murders.

"What ails you?" she asked, turned over a second card and froze, staring down at The Devil. One of the most feared cards in the deck. A predator.

She forced her mind clear, spoke aloud calmly. "What is the future?" And turned another card.

Death.

Caitlin's heart was pounding now, so loudly that she could barely hear herself think.

Many Tarot readers tried to gloss over the Death card as an indicator of change, but sometimes Death meant exactly that, and in this configuration there was nothing benign about it.

What question now? What?

"What must I watch for?" she asked, breathing deeply, and reached to turn over a new card.

The Seven of Cups. Illusion. The card she associated with shapeshifters.

Something banged behind her, and she nearly jumped out of her chair.

"Damn it." It was her sister's voice, and it came just as Shauna pushed through the curtain into the reading room and gasped, seeing Caitlin sitting at the table.

"Cait? Mother Mary, what are you doing sitting there in the dark? You just scared the living daylights out of me."

"I was just reading," Caitlin said faintly.

Shauna flipped on a light, exasperated. "I saw the shutters closed and the lights off, and I didn't think anyone was here."

"Sorry…it's…been a weird morning."

Caitlin rose and slid the cards back into the deck, then folded the deck into the silk and put it away. It was probably past time for their daily meeting.

Shauna had already breezed back into the outer shop, and when Caitlin stepped out through the curtains the shutters were wide-open, letting in the light, and Fiona was coming through the door, her arms full of flowers and a bag of cookies. Customers at A Little Bit of Magic could always count on sweet treats, not to mention champagne on holidays. The shop was a "Best of NOLA" pick every year.

Caitlin looked at her sisters, both of them exuberant, overflowing with life. Shauna was glowing from her run, and Fiona was glowing from…something else. Caitlin felt dark and distressed by comparison.

Get in that early morning tumble before the blood-sucker has to crawl back into his coffin, she thought darkly, even though technically Jagger DeFarge neither sucked blood nor slept in a coffin. Still, a Keeper being involved with a member of the race she was charged to protect was just…wrong. Cait knew that all too well.

"What's the matter?" Fiona asked her, instantly picking up on her mood.

"Bad wind," Caitlin muttered, unable to help herself.

"What?" Fiona frowned, her clear blue eyes concerned, and Shauna turned from her cash register prep to look at her.

"Something's off," Caitlin hedged. "I had a dream…and I was followed in Jackson Square this morning."

Her sisters were instantly alarmed, their voices overlapping.

"Followed?"

"Who followed you?"

"More like what," Caitlin said darkly. "Something I couldn't see. Watching me."

Her sisters didn't bother to hide the skeptical look they exchanged, and Caitlin's defenses went straight up. "And it showed up in the cards just now, too. Death and the Devil *and* the Tower. And Illusion. Shapeshifters."

Caitlin was the best card reader of all of them, but both her sisters knew enough to know that configuration was far from good. And yet, Caitlin caught another one of those exchanged glances. Caitlin knew exactly what the looks meant. *Poor Cait. She's over the top these days. Seeing shadows everywhere.*

Caitlin felt her temper flare and tried to keep a handle on it.

Fiona made it worse by being gently diplomatic about it. "Tell us what we can do, sweetie."

Caitlin now felt frustration as well as anger. "Be careful. Just be careful. When I know more, I'll tell you." She knew she sounded bitter, but how long would she have to do penance? When was she going to be able to redeem herself, set the whole vampire/shifter disaster to rest?

She found herself suddenly wishing for a cataclysm, a challenge so profound that she would be able to save herself, save everyone, and finally feel herself a true Keeper.

Shauna was already looking at the clock on the wall. "Are you going to be okay here today?" she asked. "I'm buying in Lafayette today, and Fee is meeting with Rosalyn to pick up the new Halloween costumes."

Caitlin bristled. "Why wouldn't I be okay? I can hold the fort. I'm saying *you* be careful. Both of you. Until we know more."

"We will, honey. You just call if you need anything." Fiona stepped forward and kissed her cheek, and Caitlin burned under her sweetness.

As they left, Shauna's look of pity obvious to anyone but the dead or blind, Caitlin paced the shop in a fury. She could hear them talking outside, not literally, but sometimes when the wind was blowing, she could just hear. Low, feminine murmurs now.

Shauna: Ever since the cemetery murders...

Fiona: But that's ridiculous, it wasn't Cait's fault...

Shauna: But you know Cait. If there's anything to obsess about, she's gonna obsess...

With effort, Caitlin turned off her inner ear, seething with resentment. *I'll show them. One way or another. I* will.

The morning flew by, with tourists arriving early for Halloween, coming up in just five days. There was a steady trickle of them, enticed down the short alleyway to the shop. The sugar candles were an irresistible draw, and the attraction spell the sisters had placed on the sidewalks outside didn't hurt. The least likely people drifting down Rue Royal ended up veering into their alleyway, following the burnt-sugar scent—and something less tangible but even more enticing—into the shop.

In no time it was midafternoon, and Caitlin's 3:00 p.m. Tarot reading was due any minute.

The woman who entered the shop had given her name as Amanda Peters, and she was a beauty: in her late forties, with a life force burning like a flame, lithe, auburn-haired, copper freckles on creamy skin, and a buttery Southern accent that Caitlin placed as Charlestonian.

She strode in wearing Katharine Hepburn trousers and a silky white shirt, looking like an old-style film goddess, but as soon as Caitlin led her through the velvet curtain and into the inner room and seated her in the reading chair, she dissolved into ugly, heart-rending sobs.

Love trouble, Caitlin thought wearily. *Nothing else could so completely unravel someone as strong as this.* She braced herself for the inevitable question, choked out between more sobs.

"He left me. What can I do?"

Caitlin unwrapped the cards.

She sensed that Amanda was a Wand, driven by will, so Caitlin pulled the Queen of Wands as the significator, the public mask, to represent her, then placed the cards in front of Amanda to hold and then cut. Caitlin laid out a Love Spread and turned over the first four cards.

She studied them, frowning. "Your life is in transition. The high presence of swords indicates single-minded pursuit, vengeance…."

Funny, that wasn't at all the read she had gotten from the woman herself; the cards were contradictory.

She turned to the first bar of three cards and touched her finger to the one on the far left. The King of Swords—which could indicate a dangerous, treacherous man, but with clients Caitlin always tried to start with the positive aspects of the cards. "The King of Swords is a highly intellectual, well-educated man, with a razor wit and many facets to his character. He is a natural problem-solver, but often moves on too quickly, from ideas, people and places, to provide any permanence. He can be passionate, charismatic, fascinating, challenging…and completely exhausting."

As Caitlin spoke, Amanda leaned forward on her elbows, seemingly transfixed by what Caitlin was saying. Caitlin could feel that she was reaching the woman on some profound level; she knew that look well. The other woman was hearing things that were true. "The card also represents a private person, a loner who defends his walls and boundaries fiercely. You may never get to know him no matter how long you're with him. The card also often indicates someone heavily involved in occult study…." As Caitlin continued, she was more and more aware of something wrong.

She paused and looked down at the spread again.

And then it hit her, hard. The card she had been speaking about was not the card representing Amanda's lover but was in the place of the querent: Amanda herself.

It made no sense.

She decided to deal an extra card, silently asking for clarification.

The Knight of Swords, reversed.

"This card indicates a deceitful man, treacherous and secretive beneath a surface charm…" Caitlin stopped herself. She had asked about Amanda, but again—the card indicated a deceitful man. And this time even more clearly indicated a manipulator, skilled in the occult, in glamours, in projection.

Could it be?

Caitlin bit her lip and then picked up the deck and held it as she asked the cards a quick, silent question: *What is going on here?*

She turned over a card.

Seven of Cups.

Shapeshifter.

Caitlin's head was buzzing as if it was going to explode. Across the table from her, Amanda was suddenly alert, as if sensing Caitlin's thoughts, and she started to push her chair back to stand, but too late. Caitlin lunged over the table, grabbed Amanda's wrist and held her fast as she spoke a few low, quick words. "By the powers of earth, fire, wind and sea, I command thee: unmask!"

She felt a surge of power in the arm she held, Amanda's whole body swelling with energy, a struggle. And then the woman's body shimmered—in fact, all the air in the room shimmered, there was no other word for it—and the woman's body resolved itself into...

A man.

And an amazingly handsome man, at that. Tall— very tall—broad-shouldered under a leather jacket, much bigger than she was, powerful through the chest and thighs. Longish jet-black hair curled around his ears, and he was wearing jeans worn so soft they looked like buckskin, all of which gave him a roguish, buccaneering look, decidedly unmodern.

"Well done," he commented, looking infuriatingly pleased with her.

"What are you playing at, Shifter?" Caitlin demanded, while simultaneously scanning the room behind him for a weapon. Being located down a mysterious, romantic alley was a big plus for atmosphere but not such an ideal situation when you found yourself suddenly alone with a rogue shapeshifter. And a human-form shifter, too, the most dangerous and untrustworthy kind.

"I'm not playing, Keeper. I'm not playing at all." There was a sensual menace to his voice now, which made her heart plunge in dismay.

If he meant her harm, she was in deep trouble already. She'd never seen such a complete and unexpected shift. Mentally she raced back through the encounter with the woman, racking her brain for any sign that she'd missed—a ripple, a tic, a shudder. But there had been no psychic leakage, no slipping of the form, nothing that would have signaled the presence of a shifter, much less one in assumed form. It was only the cards that had warned her.

Caitlin's mind plunged through her options. Her cell phone was in the outer shop, under the counter. The shifter was blocking the doorway to the outer shop, to the phone, to everything. There was just so much of him. And as a shapeshifter, he would be immune to any weakening spell she could have used on a human intruder; there was no point in such a spell with an Other.

"Why not just walk in and introduce yourself?" she asked, trying to keep her voice steady.

"I heard there were Keepers in town. I wanted to see how good you are." His voice made the words a lazy double entendre.

"I'm very good," she said sharply, her temper rising even in the circumstances.

"Nice to know," he said, and the laziness was gone. "You better be. There's a bad wind coming."

Now Caitlin felt a chill that had nothing to do with the man in front of her. *Bad wind. My dream. This morning.* Her own feeling, her own words.

"That's a little vague, isn't it?" she retorted. "If you've got something to say, say it."

He suddenly smiled at her, which made her even more suspicious. "I'll be glad to. I'm Ryder Mallory."

He leaned forward and extended a huge hand across the table.

She looked at him frostily. *Oh, you are, are you? As if I'm going to believe anything a shifter says.* Shapeshifters changed names as often as they changed forms.

"And?" she demanded, keeping her hands to herself.

He left his hand extended, now daring her. She felt a reluctance to take it, but what better way to sense someone out, after all? She reached across the table and touched his palm, felt her hand engulfed in his, and an electric charge…which he was no doubt aware of, because he smiled slowly and tightened his grip on her hand, not hurting her, but not letting go, either, just letting her feel the strength and heat of him.

Flustered, she pulled back, trying to extricate herself…and after another moment he let her go, but not until she was completely aware that it was only by his choice that she was free.

"Now, what do you want?" she snapped, not realizing until after she spoke that it wasn't exactly the question she'd wanted to ask.

He smiled knowingly at her. "We'll get to that. But at the moment, we have bigger fish to fry." His expression changed. "I'm a bounty hunter. I'm tracking."

"Tracking what?"

His eyes turned serious, and Caitlin felt a chill in the candlelit darkness. "There's a band of…entities on their way here. Extremely rogue. Extremely dangerous. I've been tracking them from Africa. I lost them in Antibes, but I'm guessing they're coming here next. They ride the wind."

The wind. Her bad feeling intensified, but she kept her tone skeptical. "What makes them so dangerous?"

"They weren't born into bodies of their own, so they feel no obligation to anyone human."

"No obligation to anyone? Sounds like shifters to me."

Ryder Mallory assumed a mock-injured look. "That's harsh. There are all kinds of us, you know."

"And yet, there's that one key element that distinguishes you all."

"And that would be…?"

"Your inconstancy."

He looked at her piercingly, and Caitlin suddenly felt naked, wanting to run. "Ah," he said. "You've been hurt."

"Isn't that your nature?" she whipped back at him.

"Tell me who it is and I'll take care of him," he said, and he sounded completely serious.

"Why assume it's a *him?*" Her temper flared.

He fixed her with a look that set her insides on

fire. "Some things are obvious without the cards, Keeper."

"Who hired you?" she demanded, trying to get back on track.

His face suddenly closed off. "That's confidential."

"And why should I believe anything a shifter says?"

"That's your job, isn't it? To determine these things? You said you were good." He held her gaze, and it was intimate in the small room, more intimate than she wanted it to be, enough to make her breath short.

She forced herself to focus, to keep her voice steady. "Thanks for the warning. I'll be sure to look out for…entities. Do you have a number where I can reach you?"

"I'm at the Marie Claire." It was a small, older hotel, just a few blocks away.

"And you know where to find me, obviously," she said.

"I do." There was a sensual promise in his voice that she didn't want to acknowledge, so she just stared coldly.

"Then I think we're done, here," she said, and hoped it would be enough of a hint to get him out.

"It's been a pleasure." He rose to leave, and was about to exit through the velvet curtain, when he turned. "Good reading, by the way—in case I didn't say." He paused, with a slight smile. "Did I tell you I read cards, too?"

He reached for the deck still facedown on the table, fanned out the cards, and his hand hovered briefly before he reached casually and turned one over.

Caitlin stared down at it. The Lovers.

Ryder Mallory smiled into her eyes, a slow, infuriating smile.

"I'll be in touch—Keeper."

He brushed out through the purple curtain, and Caitlin stood, frozen, not breathing, until she heard the outer door open and close.

Then she jerked forward and swept the cards up into their silk wrapper, slammed the cupboard door on them and pushed out through the curtain.

The daylight of the shop was nearly blinding after the candlelit cocoon of the reading room, and Caitlin blinked to adjust. Her brain was roiling with confusion and anger.

She stalked behind the counter and grabbed for her cell phone, started punching the speed-dial for Fiona…

Then stopped, and forced herself to breathe.

They didn't believe you this morning, so what makes you think they would believe you now?

She set the phone down, thinking.

This time I'm going to do it right.

Then she turned and walked to the front window, turned the Open sign to Closed, and hurried out the door.

Chapter 3

Caitlin hurried down the uneven cobblestone sidewalks of Royal. Air-conditioning blasted from the open doors, cooling the sidewalks enough to entice shoppers inside.

The wind, which had been quiet for most of the day, was picking up again, warm and gusting, swirling flurries of glittering dust up from the streets.

Bad wind, Caitlin thought again, and then was angry at herself for using the shapeshifter's words, even though she'd said them first.

The Eighth District New Orleans Police Department was located in the heart of the Quarter, just four blocks away from the shop, and it and the courthouse took up two square city blocks all on their own. It was, Caitlin thought, probably the most magnificent police station in the country: a massive three-tiered white-and-gray-veined marble wedding cake of a building, with grand old magnolia trees in the yard and tall black wrought-iron fences. Even in such a formal setting, the mysterious beauty of New Orleans carried the day.

Tourists and locals alike were drawn to take rest on its sweeping marble steps, and could be found day and night, lounging back on their elbows, under the shade of blossoming magnolias, as street musicians and singers played to their captive and willing audience from the sidewalk on the other side of the street.

Caitlin hurried up the steps, past a group of Goth teenagers watching a couple of the boys on skateboards do whatever they called those flip things on the stairs.

Across the street, a saxophonist played a sultry version of "Georgia," the notes enticingly full and sexy. Caitlin turned and glanced at him. The well-muscled Jamaican tipped his head to her as he played.

She turned and hurried up the stairs.

And on the sidewalk, concealed in his musician body, Ryder watched her, his lips wrapped around the mouthpiece of the horn.

This is interesting, he thought, as he lowered the

sax, staring at the police station. He'd known back at the shop that the indifference the Keeper had been demonstrating to his story was completely feigned. She might be distrustful of him, but she certainly believed that there was danger in the city; that had come through loud and clear in her thoughts. The focus of her concern had also been clear—her sisters above all else, which was also interesting. Ryder wondered if there had already been some kind of attack, or if she'd sensed some sort of menace, that would make her so instantly jumpy.

But she hadn't done the obvious thing, which would have been to run to her sisters, the other Keepers, who were, in Ryder's experience and at least in other parts of the world, notoriously clannish. He had been counting on taking on some sweet, innocent form to make it easier to eavesdrop. A cat was always good for women—and he wouldn't have minded curling up in Caitlin MacDonald's lap, either.

Instead, here she was, going straight to the police, which was not necessarily in Ryder's best interests, not by a long shot—but it meant she knew something. And he intended to find out what.

Beautiful as this Caitlin was—*those silver eyes*—she was only a means to an end. He would follow where she led only as long as it was useful, and no longer.

He stepped into the stairwell where he'd left the

unconscious street musician while he stole his form and his sax, gently deposited the sax on the step beside him, and let his own face change again.

Inside the police department, Caitlin passed impatiently through security, gathered the belongings she'd had to send through the X-ray machine—shoes, belt, jewelry—and pulled them back on, then raced down the hall toward the Homicide Division.

She forced herself to slow down, then stopped, hovering outside in the doorway. Seated at a prime desk in the detectives' bullpen was her future brother-in-law, homicide detective Jagger DeFarge.

Jagger looked like a rugged, exceptionally attractive man. In reality he was not a man at all. Caitlin had been horrified when Fiona—who had always been the steady one, the most rational sister, the one who'd fought to keep the family together ever since their parents' deaths ten years ago—fell in love with the vampire. There was no outright ban against Keepers intermarrying with Others, but separation was part of a long tradition, and to Caitlin the idea would have seemed unnatural even if such an intermarriage hadn't led to the long and bloody battle that had cost her parents their lives. While Others fought in the streets of New Orleans, ripping each other apart with claw and fang, Liam and Jen MacDonald had summoned all the powers they possessed to cast a circle of peace....

The effort had killed them both.

How could Fiona forget that? Our parents died *because a few Others couldn't keep to their own kind.*

And then there was the whole "cemetery murders" disaster. If Caitlin herself hadn't been enmeshed in a secret and totally disastrous interspecies relationship of her own...

But I cut it off, Caitlin told herself. *And I'm never going there again. Ever.*

She forced her mind back to the problem of Jagger DeFarge.

Jagger was a good cop, and even, Caitlin had to admit—reluctantly—to all intents and purposes a good man. In fact, he had saved her own life as well as Fiona's when the "vampire killers" had held them hostage in a crypt.

But she still didn't trust him—with anything, much less her sister. Fiona deserved the best.

Her ace in the hole was that *she* knew that *Jagger* knew he had not yet won her over, which meant he would bend over backward to help her in the hope of scoring brownie points. Which made him useful right now.

Caitlin took a breath and stepped through the doorway. Jagger was behind his desk in the bullpen, writing some report with a scowl of concentration. But at Caitlin's first step into the room he looked up

sharply—that annoying sixth sense of a vampire—
then rose to his feet instantly as he saw her with
equally annoying grace, an elegance just a little too
good to be real. Or human.

Damn vampires.

"Caitlin," he said, and moved around his desk to
her side. "Nothing wrong, I hope." The concern in
his voice was genuine; Caitlin knew he was thinking
of Fiona, worried that something had happened to
her.

"No, not really," she said ambiguously, knowing
he would bite. So to speak. "I was just wondering
if there had been any—" she paused, pretended to
search for words "—any unusual activity in the city
recently. I don't know…a spike in crime…murders,
maybe…"

Jagger looked at her so sharply that she knew she
had her answer. She felt a prickle of excitement but
kept her face carefully neutral.

"Why would you ask that?" He was all cop now,
not a trace of future brother-in-law in sight.

Caitlin put on her most innocent, spacey, younger
sister frown. "I had a very bad Tarot reading this
morning." *Well, it was true, wasn't it?* "I came to
you because I thought you might know, and if you
didn't, I thought maybe you *should* know."

Jagger studied her, and she knew he was perplexed.
That's fine, be perplexed. But he knew she was a

Keeper, and he would not be inclined to dismiss her premonitions and readings; keeping watch on the town was her job, by ancient decree, just as much as it was Fiona's. Caitlin decided to push just a little bit harder. She let her lip tremble appealingly. "I guess I shouldn't have asked. I'm sorry." She turned toward the door to go.

Behind her, Jagger said, "As a matter of fact, there's been a string of drug deaths. It looks like a bad batch of meth."

Caitlin turned slowly, and this time she studied *his* face. It was clear that wasn't the whole story. "But…" she prompted.

"But…" His eyes fixed hers intently, and for a moment she felt guilty for manipulating him. "There's something off about the lab reports, and it's been bothering me."

"Hmm. Drugs. I didn't see anything about drugs in the cards." She frowned in concentration, while inside she remembered the Devil card, which had been in the center of the spread. Of all the cards, it was the strongest indicator of addiction, of dangerous substances. But she wasn't about to say that.

"I did get the Illusion card," she pondered aloud. "It was prominent in the spread. Illusion often means addiction. Alcohol. Drugs." She was improvising for Jagger's benefit—she'd already gotten all she needed to know.

"Well…as long as you're on top of it, I won't worry too much," she concluded brightly. "I'll see you back at the compound, I guess."

As she turned to go, Jagger said her name with such quiet force that she had to turn. "Cait."

He looked into her face, and she had to stop herself from squirming. "Please keep me informed—if you get any more signs."

"Oh, I will," she assured him sweetly. "You'll be the first to know."

Not, she added silently as she headed for the door.

In the hall outside, she could barely contain her elation. She had a real clue now with the drug deaths.

I can do this. I can figure it out on my own. I don't need anyone at all.

Because if whatever was going on had anything to do with drugs, she knew exactly where to go to find out.

Chapter 4

Bourbon Street.

New Orleans' most famous tourist attraction, the sleazy, noisy, rowdy, free-for-all strip that stretched fourteen blocks from Canal Street almost to Esplanade. It was closed to automobile traffic every night of the week so tourists and revelers could walk unimpeded down the rough pavement, taking in the street performers, dodging—or inviting—the bead-throwing partiers on the balconies above, dropping in through the wide-open doors of every music club, strip club, bar, souvenir shop, voodoo shop and sex toy shop along the way. Bourbon was a wild and woolly, nonstop circus of decadence and indulgence.

Caitlin hated it.

There were so many pleasures in New Orleans, sensual and otherwise, that were so much more complicated and rewarding than boorish Bourbon… although it did serve the purpose of keeping the more obnoxious visitors to NOLA confined in one easily avoidable part of the city.

What fewer people knew was that Bourbon was where many of the city's shapeshifters naturally gravitated. More obviously, it was also the drug capital of the Quarter.

Before venturing up to Bourbon, Caitlin waited for dark, since the shifters she meant to call on rarely showed their faces before sunset. And that gave her time to go back to the shop and dress for the occasion…in a glamour.

A glamour was one of Caitlin's favorite spells. Not everyone could do it, but she was a quick study, and she'd had a good teacher…but she wasn't going to think about that.

Standing in front of a full-length mirror by the light of the moon helped but wasn't mandatory. In a pinch, the light of a candle did nicely. What *was* mandatory was the relaxation, the becoming conscious of every part of her body…and then focusing particularly on the whole of her skin. She looked into the mirror and breathed slowly, keenly aware of the glow of the candlelight on her…until she began to feel the glow as photons of light, a rain of warmth over her entire body. She began to chant softly:

"Light pass through me, no one will see me. Light pass through me, no one will see me. Light pass through me, no one will see me…"

She chanted and stared into the mirror, focusing on the light, until the borders of her silhouette became hazy, insubstantial, until her whole body started wavering, like the warm flickering of a candle flame…until all she could see in the mirror was light.

And then she could see the cabinet behind her, as if she was no longer there. She felt, not saw, herself smile, and said softly to herself, "Everything seen and those not seen, let me walk now in between. As I say, so mote it be!"

She turned, invisibly, and walked toward the door.

On Bourbon, Caitlin strode through the crowds clogging the street with no fear of the prowling pickpockets and the inevitable drunk men who would have been hitting on her, hitting hard, had she not been protected by the cloak of the glamour. She loved the power of walking invisible as the air, through the warring music blasting from the wide-open doors of the clubs: Zydeco; karaoke; slow, sultry jazz…

The street looked, as always, like a stage set. There was something about the flatness of it, she thought—being able to see for blocks and blocks, and the balconies of revelers up above…there was a Shakespearean flavor to everything that she had to admit was appealing…especially when you were invisible.

She was entirely unnoticed by the drunk revelers, the break-tap-dancing teenagers…the buskers holding signs advertising Huge Ass Beers To Go and the opposing signs waved by religious crazies: God Punishes All Sinners. Caitlin squeezed quickly by the sign wielders, grimacing…. Then, as she was passing a blind street musician wearing sunglasses à la Ray Charles, he stepped right in her path and bowed, a breathtakingly courtly gesture, and spoke. "Lovely lady."

Caitlin froze, as confused as the crowd of tourists around her, who looked around them with comic double-takes, having no idea who or what the musician was talking to, unable to even wrap their minds around the idea that he was seeing anyone at all. It could all just have been part of the show to them.

No big surprise, Caitlin told herself. There were psychics of all kinds in NOLA—either the city drew them or actually bred them—and it wasn't much of a stretch that a blind man would have learned to use other senses.

But she had her own mission, so she quickly sidestepped the jazzman and continued on into the crowd.

Behind her on the sidewalk, Ryder straightened in his Ray Charles body, swept up the hat containing his tips, and followed her at a distance, tapping his cane for show.

The glamour was a good one, he would give her that. It demonstrated as high a level of skill as unmasking him in the shop earlier that day had done. If this Keeper's sisters were as good as she was, there was a strong Keeper presence in the city, as strong as he'd seen in any town for a long time…as strong as their parents' had been rumored to be.

That didn't mean he trusted her. She had issues, this one, obviously. But she might be useful, down the line. And she was on a mission tonight—first the vampire detective, now this obvious continuance of her investigation, which, whatever it was, required a glamour. Which made it his business to investigate.

Besides, invisible as she may have been to the others around them, for him, the view from behind wasn't bad at all.

Ryder was enjoying being on Bourbon again. The sights and sounds were intoxicating…neon lights in all colors and the sparkling, feathered costumes of the revelers…the long, sleek legs of the showgirls, the bright, glazed eyes of the tourists, the smells of chocolate and piña coladas….

His impulse was to follow every impulse.

Instead he focused and followed Caitlin.

Caitlin weaved forward through the crowd, her jaw now clenched grimly. It was probably the influence of Halloween coming up, but it was barely nine o'clock and the partiers seemed even more out of control than usual. The drunk guy on the balcony to her right, blatantly taking camera phone shots of his girlfriend's crotch. The college crowd on the left balcony dangling beads off the railing, shouting "Show me your tits!" and "Give me sumpin'!" to everyone passing by. The stumbling drunk bridal parties, one group right now passing Caitlin with a sullen bride in the middle wearing a T-shirt reading I'm The Bride, Those Are The Bitches.

And Caitlin knew it was just beginning. As the night and the *bon temps* rolled on, more and more people would be holding their friends up as they stumbled from one bar to the next, stopping to partake of every "Huge Ass Beer!" and Hurricane and Hand Grenade and Jello shot offered to them. I Got Bourbon-Faced On Shit Street T-shirts were popular souvenirs for a reason. So many wasted lives—literally.

Caitlin put on speed as she saw her goal ahead of her. The music literally rocked her as she approached;

Bons Temps was one of the loudest clubs on Bourbon, and that was saying a lot.

She stepped through the doors and saw that there was a cover band up on stage, and even at this decibel range, the musical talent was obvious; the best musicians flocked to New Orleans just as surely as they did to Nashville and L.A.

These particular musicians, no surprise, were clearly altered: drunk, stoned, high.

Wasted.

The lead singer, Case, had a falsetto to rival Steve Connor and an Iggy Pop tilt to his slim hips; in his bandanna and artfully ripped T-shirt, he was a pirate who expertly twirled the mike in his fingers and charmed the female patrons with a mad and manic gleam in his eyes. The very young keyboard player, Danny, wore a Megadeth T-shirt and looked like an angel with his long, shimmering hair and beatific face…until you noticed his completely empty eyes.

Caitlin's stomach heaved, and she had to turn away from the stage.

The floor was always packed at Bons Temps; no other Bourbon Street club was so crowded, so consistently. Not just because the guys were great musicians; they were, but there was a little something extra. When Case sang Aerosmith, sometimes you could swear you were looking at Steven Tyler. A Police number? It might have been that third Hurricane, but sometimes you would bet your life it was a young Sting up there singing. Eminem, Bono, Flo Rida... it was a subtle thing, but wildly effective with the drunk crowds....

Because Case and Danny were shapeshifters. The most skilled species: shifters whose expertise was taking on different human forms.

And Caitlin had a long and ambiguous acquaintance with these two shifters.

Shapeshifters were rarely productive members of society; their sense of self was too amorphous, and because of that inconstancy and lack of center, they tended toward indulgences of all kinds. But they were also wildly charismatic, in no small part because they could subtly alter their physical form to match other people's fantasies, and they were often excellent psychics, because they passed through the astral, a parallel dimension of spirits and entities, easily used for transportation between planes of reality, every time they shifted. And in the astral, all kinds of things could be gleaned: past, present and future.

The rowdy lead singer, Case, was the charismatic. But Danny...Danny was the psychic. One of New Orleans' best, which was saying a hell of a lot—that is, when he was straight enough to concentrate, which was almost never, these days.

Wasted, Caitlin thought again. *Such a waste.*

She pulled her eyes away from Danny and concentrated on Case: skinny as Keith Richards, for the same reasons, in pencil-leg black jeans, sporting alligator boots with outrageously long toes. He was leaning into the crowd with Danny now, threatening to topple off the stage into the throng, and shouting, "Somebody freakin' scream!"

And then, as he straightened, his eyes fell on the corner where Caitlin stood…and he stopped for an instant, staring. Then his smile curved.

Caitlin thought, *He's good.* He saw her. Of course he did; he always could. She let the glamour slip away from her like a cloak, and he gazed full into her face. Then he lifted the mike again and shouted, "Somebody make some noise!"

As the crowd went wild on the floor beneath him, he turned the mike over to the guitarist for a solo and dropped off the stage, landing hard on those ridiculous boots and swaggering out into the crowd, stopping to let some drunk sorority girl kiss him, openmouthed and sloppy.

Caitlin turned away and walked out the back door, into the small inner courtyard, away from the noise. The courtyard was mostly used for storage. Cases of booze were stacked to the eaves against the inner wall, but there was a small outdoor bar, framed by white strings of Christmas lights, tonight unmanned and deserted.

Case pushed out through the double doors and into

the dark. He was already flicking a Zippo, lighting a cigarette, dragging hard, and Caitlin wondered wearily what it would be laced with tonight.

As if hearing her thoughts, he extended the cigarette toward her mockingly. She stared at him, ignoring his outstretched hand, and history vibrated between them like an electric pulse.

Finally he smiled. "Ah, the little Keeper. Sister Goldenhair Surprise. Nice glamour, by the way. You're getting good at that. We'll have you full-tilt shifting any day now."

Her anger flared, and she answered without thinking. "Not in this lifetime."

He gave her a "We'll see" smile and dragged on his cigarette. "Well, Keeper, has someone been bad?" He asked the question slyly, and she jolted. *So he does know something,* she thought, trying to conceal her excitement.

"Why would you say that?" she answered, unconsciously echoing Jagger DeFarge.

"Someone must have been pretty bad, to bring you up to our little den of iniquity. Or is that *din?*" he corrected himself, reaching to his ears and pulling out earplugs, the only thing that had kept him from going deaf for all these years.

"I need…" She hesitated.

"My help?" His eyes gleamed at her.

"Some information," she said coldly.

"You're in luck. I'm running a special tonight." He sat back on a bar stool, legs spread casually—nothing to do with the conversation, of course.

Caitlin's heart turned over with the old, familiar pain, then she answered back, sharp and hard. "Good thing I've got credit running into the next century, then."

To her surprise, he laughed aloud, and she realized with relief that with that comeback she had scored—enough to keep him playing along, at least for a while. "There are people dying of some kind of bad batch," she said quickly, while he was still smiling. "Meth, the police think."

His eyes widened innocently. "'Just Say No.'"

She ignored that. "I want to know if you know anything about it."

Caitlin suddenly noticed there was a bartender behind the bar now, a young kid, college age, with good enough instincts not to hover; he was quietly restocking the shelves. Case snapped at him, "Jack and Cokes over here," and waited until the kid turned away to answer Caitlin.

"What about drugs don't I know?" he quipped. "But it's only tourists who are dying, sugar. NHI."

NHI was a cop insult referring to the lowest of lowlifes: No Humans Involved. Of course, in New Orleans that could get confusing....

"Just tourists," Caitlin echoed, pondering.

"Drug virgins," Case elaborated helpfully. "Couldn't handle the high."

But why? Caitlin wondered. *Tourists doing meth? It didn't make sense.*

The young bartender set drinks in front of them. Caitlin ignored hers, while Case drained his in one pull.

Behind the bar, cloaked as the college kid, Ryder bided his time. It was taking everything he had to conceal his disgust for Case, for the scene playing out before him. Classic Shifter, this one, taking full advantage of his glamours, which wouldn't work on an Other, obviously, but humans fell for them every time. And Keepers, too, it looked like. Even with her specialized knowledge, Caitlin had been ensnared, at least at one time. *And by what? This pathetic excuse for an Other, so enamored of his powers that he's lost all sense of who he ever was—the center cannot hold. And a drunk and an addict on top of that, clearly.*

"Do you know a shifter named Ryder Mallory?" Caitlin asked suddenly, and Ryder was jarred out of his thoughts. Did she sense him?

He moved casually down the bar to get out of her range, crouched as if to reach under the sink.

Case stared at Caitlin, lifted an eyebrow. "Can't say that I do." He reached in front of her for her drink, lifted and drained it.

Lying, Caitlin thought. *Not even bothering to cover.*

He smiled at her, as if reading her thoughts. "Can't keep track of everyone, *cher.*"

"Well, if anything comes to you, you'll tell me, I'm sure," she said.

"I'd rather come to *you, cher.* In you, with you, in every which way," Case said softly, and leaned over to lift a strand of hair from her cheek, curling it around his finger, tugging her forward….

Behind the bar, Ryder abruptly stood, anger flaring, and in that moment Case turned sharply and stared toward him. Ryder adjusted his body, struggled to hold the cloak of illusion in place…and once again he was just a college kid, merely spacing out in Case's direction.

After a long moment Case turned back to Caitlin, but Ryder could see that the younger shapeshifter was jumpy now, and figured he'd better get while the getting was good. He couldn't afford to be caught, at least until he knew more. He picked up a case of Turbodog and headed for the kitchen door.

Caitlin didn't know what had just gone on, but Case was suddenly edgy and hyper.

"Got to get back," he said, jerking his head in the general direction of the stage. "My public awaits."

"I want to talk to Danny," she said abruptly.

She saw Case stiffen subtly, but he covered it well, smiled at her. "Why would that be, Keeper?"

There was no point in lying to him; he always knew. "I want a sitting. To see what he's seen out there." She knew Case would know she didn't mean on the streets but in the astral.

Case shook his head mockingly. "Danny's not home tonight."

Meaning Danny was high, as if she didn't know. Her anger burned. "How do you live with yourself?" she asked, not bothering to hide her contempt.

"Same way Danny does, *cher*. One hit at a time."

Too angry to speak, she turned and stalked for the door.

His voice came from the dark behind her, mocking. "Rough night out there. Don't forget your glamour."

She faced him stoically. He was right, of course.

He stared across the dark courtyard, into her eyes. "And don't forget—I taught you that, little sister."

"Yes," she heard herself saying bitterly. "You taught me a lot."

She turned again and was gone.

Inside the club, she leaned against the wall in the narrow hallway and breathed deeply until she could focus enough to pull the glamour back on.

The music was blasting, but strangely, the rhythm

made the glamour easier to conjure. When she straightened away from the wall, the drunk bridesmaids who tumbled by her en route to the bathroom didn't even give her a glance.

Caitlin weaved her way across the crowded floor. On stage, Danny was at the piano, hair shimmering like dark water over his shoulders, beautiful and empty-eyed. Caitlin turned away, disturbed…and caught a glimpse of Case standing on the dance floor in front of the stage. He suddenly crouched down, dropping out of sight. Caitlin stopped, craning to see what was going on. He was on his haunches talking very seriously to a blonde little girl of maybe five, sporting a rakish, sequined hat. As the little girl watched, enthralled, Case twirled a drumstick between his fingers and then extended the drumstick toward her.

She took it and without hesitation twirled the stick in imitation. As Case laughed, his whole face transformed.

Caitlin blinked back tears and fled the club.

Chapter 5

Once out in the kaleidoscopic cacophony of the street, Caitlin realized she was so shaky she could barely hold the glamour in place. She always felt that way, seeing Case. And Danny, too. Her feelings for them were so complex.… Longing, despair, anger, protectiveness…

And failure. As shifters, they were her charges, and not only had she been manipulated and controlled by the very people she was supposed to have charge of, she hadn't helped them. Not a bit.

She took long breaths, forcing the spell to stabilize.

Part of the trouble was that she had known Case

forever, it seemed, since she was just a teenager. As the middle MacDonald child, she'd had a rebellious streak. Fiona was *so* good, *so* perfect, and Shauna so outgoing and loved, and their parents had been such pillars of the community, *all* the communities. Caitlin never felt she could live up to any of them. So she found relief by sneaking out of the house, out of the compound, up to big bad Bourbon Street, to listen to music, drink the Hurricanes that older guys would buy her....

Case had saved her from a bad situation one night, when a drunker than usual frat boy thought that buying Caitlin a drink meant anything went, including date rape. Of course, that turned out to be the proverbial "out of the frying pan, into the fire" scenario in the end, but at first Case had been so charming, as rebellious as Caitlin herself, but also a naturally talented shifter as well as singer, and very willing to teach her. She had spent many hours after-hours in clubs, listening to Case and Danny jamming with their band of the moment, and learning the shortcuts of shapeshifting.

Then came the War, and her parents' deaths had devastated Caitlin and her sisters. Caitlin, in particular, had been consumed by guilt. She'd taken her parents for granted, had gone behind their backs, and now she could never make up for any of it. In her zeal to reform she had become completely devoted to her sisters, obedient to Fiona and fiercely protective of Shauna.

Caitlin had kept her distance from Case as well as she could, as the three MacDonald sisters had thrown themselves into the grueling task of building the trust and connection with the communities of Others that their parents had had.

But in recent years she had been increasingly disturbed by rumors of his drug use—Danny's, too. Rumors that they had fallen prey to the drugs and disillusion that claimed so many shifters. Caitlin had tried to intervene, in her official capacity as a Keeper. But old feelings proved overwhelming. She'd slipped and reconnected with Case, wanting to believe his stories of being clean, of reforming…only to be horrified to discover the extent of his new addictions. She had pressured and badgered and ranted, and then sunk into despair, all the time hiding it from her sisters, until, ironically, it was Case who dumped her, unable to take her condemnation.

That had been just before a series of nightgown-clad blondes started turning up in New Orleans cemeteries, bodies drained of blood.

If Caitlin's brain hadn't been so scrambled, she surely would have seen the killer for what it really was. Instead, because of her confusion, her inattention, both she and Fiona had almost been killed….

And Caitlin had been living with that guilt, ever since.

But I'm going to do it right, this time, she vowed.

She straightened, squaring her shoulders, and moved down the crowded street, slipping like water around the drunken revelers—frat boys, businessmen, pimps.

The noise of the street was overwhelming, distracting, and she turned down a side street, heading for quieter Rue Royal so she could hear herself think. She was past the Rainbow line, St. Ann Street, where hetero clubs turned gay and the side streets turned seedier, but she had on the glamour and Royal was just one long block down.

Even so, she instinctively walked a little more quickly as she brooded over the clearest clue she had gotten from Case: these were *tourists* dropping dead, not junkies. *Tourists doing meth?* No wonder Jagger was perturbed. And despite his nonchalance, she could tell even Case thought it was strange.

Caitlin was so deep in thought that she didn't notice the footsteps until they were right up on her—heavy, pounding, manic—and before she could even turn, a heavy, live, stinking weight had tackled her, hurling her to the ground.

She hit the pavement so hard that her breath was knocked out of her and she heard as well as felt her head crack against the curb, and the pain was blinding; through the haze, she knew for the first time what it was like to see stars. Through her confusion she thought, *How can he see me? Who is this?*

Despite overwhelming pain, Caitlin heaved herself up and called on a weakening spell, something quick and forceful to stun her attacker.

She gathered energy in her mind and *shoved*....

The assailant—she had just enough time to register a Bourbon-Faced T-shirt and a man's face so distorted with rage it barely looked human—growled like a bear and tackled her again.

Not human, Caitlin realized. *He's Other.* And then she hit the sidewalk again, was crushed into the cobblestones.

Whoever was on top of her was so heavy she couldn't move, couldn't breathe, and the smell was strange. Under the familiar sick-sweetness of too many Hurricanes was not the reek of human sweat, but something like ammonia, and then there were hands around her neck, squeezing, squeezing, and through the pain and descending blackness she realized she was being killed....

Panicked thoughts flooded her brain. She would never see her sisters again, never meet the love of her life....

So this is how it ends....

And then suddenly she felt the pressure lift and gulped in air....

* * *

Ryder seized the man in the Bourbon Street T-shirt in a full-out fury and hauled him off Caitlin. The attacker snarled and spun on Ryder, hulking and wired with superhuman strength. He was dressed like a tourist, but the face was a mask of inhuman rage, and beneath the innocuous jeans and T-shirt he was completely out of control, like someone on PCP and steroids at the same time, some drug-crazed, murderous, rapacious zombie.

Ryder seized the tourist by the scruff of his "Bourbon-Faced" T-shirt and slammed him against the side of the voodoo shop beside them. The tourist's head hit the wall with a sickening thud. But the man merely roared and barreled forward again. Ryder sidestepped, grabbed the man's arm and used his own momentum against him to snap the bone.

On the pavement behind them, Caitlin flinched as she heard the crack of her attacker's arm breaking. The limb dropped against his side at an unnatural angle, but even with blood streaming from his head and the useless, dangling arm, he seemed to be feeling no pain at all. He roared again and scuttled off, listing to one side.

Ryder sprinted back to where Caitlin was crumpled on the street, stooped and picked her up in his arms as if she weighed nothing, and strode across the sidewalk to set her carefully up against the wall of the nearest shop. He knelt in front of her and took her face in his hands, looked into her eyes. She could feel the heat of him, the adrenaline of the fight—and more—a molten anger, which she realized, startled, was rage that she'd been attacked. "Are you hurt?" he demanded.

She swallowed, overwhelmed.

"Caitlin," he said roughly. "Do you know who I am?"

"Who?" she answered weakly. It was a joke, but he seemed to take it seriously.

"Do you know where you are?" he asked more urgently.

"St. Ann Street," she answered meekly.

"What day is it?"

"Thursday. I'm fine," she protested and started to struggle to her feet. Ryder took her firmly by the waist and sat her down again, and she gasped, not from pain, but from the electrically sexual feeling of his hands on her. Heat suddenly pulsed through her entire body.

It's adrenaline, that's all. You just almost died, of course you've got a rush, she told herself.

He took her face in his hands and leaned over her, and she went light-headed, sure he was going to kiss her. But he only turned her head gently to one side, then the other, examining her throat. She felt limp in his hands, overwhelmed with the chemistry of their contact.

Suddenly he was still, no longer examining her but just looking into her eyes. His were green as the sea.

"Keeper," he said, and his voice was hoarse. His eyes looked into her, through her, and this time his thumbs brushed her lips, sending another electric current through her…. She could feel the rise and fall of his chest, and she knew that whatever she was feeling, he was feeling it, too….

Abruptly he pulled back, looked down the street. "I don't have much time. That guy will be dead in minutes. I have to get to him first." He gripped her arms once again. "I'll be back for you."

Before she could speak, he was on his feet and sprinting down the street in the direction the tourist had gone.

Caitlin slammed her palms on the sidewalk and pushed herself up. "The hell with that," she muttered aloud.

She staggered, dizzy, and had to hold herself up on the wall…then tore off down the street after him.

The next block was empty and dark. Down the street Caitlin could see Ryder barreling after the tourist, who was moving fast but stumbling like a drunk zombie.

Ryder put on a burst of speed, long, hard-muscled

legs pumping, but before he could tackle the tourist, the man did a sudden spin—and then his body jack-knifed backward, his spine arching until his head nearly touched his ass. Caitlin stopped in her tracks with a gasp of horror. Then the tourist jerked again, his chest bulging as if his heart was about to break free.

He was making choking noises, foaming at the mouth, as his body bowed backward and forward in horrific contortions.

Either this is a massive heart attack or an alien is about to burst out through his ribs, Caitlin thought wildly.

And then there was the sound of a siren approaching, followed by feet pounding, and she was seized around the waist as Ryder grabbed her and hauled her back into a storefront, holding her against his side.

A patrol car skidded around the corner, past the doorway where they were hiding. Uniformed cops were jumping out even before the vehicle came to a complete stop.

The cops ran for the tourist, who did one final, impossible jackknife and collapsed in the middle of the street.

The cops surrounded him with weapons drawn.

"Hands behind your head!" one shouted. The tourist didn't move.

"Put your hands behind your head!" the officer repeated grimly.

The body lay still. The uniforms advanced cautiously, weapons at the ready.

At Ryder's side, Caitlin strained to see around the corner of the doorway. In death, a shapeshifter's body returned to its original form, and she wanted to see what that original form was.

The tourist's head had dropped to the side, and his face was angled straight toward the doorway where she and Ryder stood. The streetlamps provided a perfectly lit view. Cait held her breath, waiting for the change….

The tourist's eyes were wide and staring. Definitely dead.

But his features remained the same, as did the proportions of his body. Caitlin shook her head, not understanding. "But…"

Ryder said quietly beside her, "He wasn't a shapeshifter."

Chapter 6

Caitlin grabbed Ryder's arm with a ferocity that she could tell startled him. "Then what *was* he? I want to know *now*," she demanded—then stopped dead as he put his fingers on her mouth and she felt a tingle in her lips, again that raw, aching electricity.

"Shh," he said against her face. "We need to get out of here first. That vampire friend of yours will be here any second."

"He's not my—"

Before she could finish, he was taking her arm and moving her back into the narrow alley between the shops, away from the gathering crowd of police.

The iron gate to the courtyard was padlocked,

but Ryder did something with some kind of tool he pulled from an inside pocket of his leather coat, and the lock clicked open. Once they were through, he reached back through the bars and snapped the lock shut before taking her arm again to move into the darkness of the inner courtyard. This time Caitlin pulled her arm away and grabbed for the tool in his hand.

He let her take it, amused, and watched her as she examined it greedily. He could still feel the softness of her lips on his fingertips and entertained the thought of kissing that mouth, of forcing those lush lips open and plunging his tongue into her, hearing her moan and soften under him as he pulled her hips against his….

She looked up from the device, frowning. It was a skeleton key, nothing more than that. "Is it enchanted?"

"Just a little."

Her eyes narrowed, and he could tell she wanted it. He pressed his advantage. "You can have it—if we can talk."

She clenched her jaw, but he could tell he had her. "If you talk first," she agreed sullenly.

"Deal," he said.

The key got them through two more back doors and a front gate, and then they were on St. Philip Street.

Ryder turned to Caitlin and presented her with the key with a mock bow. She narrowed her eyes again and then snatched it from his hand. To his delight, she pulled a little bag from her cleavage, which he recognized as a gris-gris pouch, a voodoo charm bag, and dropped the key in, before returning the bag to the enticing cleft between her breasts. *First the key and then me,* he thought, and felt himself stir in anticipation.

She suddenly blushed as if she'd read his thoughts. Before she could turn away, he grabbed her hand and felt her pull back from him—but just a little. "Now we talk, that's the deal. How about Maguire's?" he said, hoping the tavern was still there.

She looked startled. "It hasn't been Maguire's for almost a hundred years. It's called the Mississippi River Bottom, now…." She frowned. "How did you know…?" Then she stopped, and after a moment she nodded warily.

The tavern had two entrances—one on the street and one off the side courtyard. Ryder moved through the side gates to the courtyard automatically; that had been the main door when last he'd visited the place.

He looked around curiously. There were neon bar signs hung on the brick, but the building was still the same, and the old twisted tree still grew out of an ancient brick planter, though bigger now than ever.

"Hasn't changed," he said aloud, approvingly.

"Since when?" she asked, watching him warily.

"Eighteen…" He paused. "Eighteen eighty-four, it was."

Caitlin looked at him, jolted. Shapeshifters weren't immortal, like vampires, but every time they passed through the astral it arrested the aging process, so a shifter who was able to shift often, providing he was able to stay out of other kinds of trouble, could live a long, long life.

If Mallory was telling the truth—always a big "if" when you were dealing with a shifter—he was very good and had been around for a very long time. *It must be lonely,* she found herself thinking.

He was still lost in reverie. "This used to be a brothel, you know. Sweet little thing named Marie hanged herself from that tree when her sailor man came back in a coffin."

Another jolt. Caitlin knew that story—it was a staple of the local ghost tours. But Ryder actually sounded as if he'd known her….

"Some guides say you can still feel the energy from—" she started.

But she never got to finish, because he turned to her and said, "Let's find out," just before he pulled her toward him and kissed her.

Heat flooded through her instantly, from her lips to the very core of her; she felt she'd just burst into flame. She opened her mouth—to protest or sigh, she didn't know which—and his tongue was inside her mouth, tasting, teasing, entwining with hers, and then plunging, sliding so deep that she lost her balance. He caught her, lifted her up and set her on the low wall around the tree, bending her backward so he could crush her mouth under his. Her back was against the trunk, and he was stepping between her legs, pulling her hips forward against his, as he kissed her, deep and slow and hot, cupping her breasts in his hands. Her nipples strained through her dress against his palms, and now he moaned, and lifted his head to kiss down her neck, biting, sucking, until she lost her breath and turned to jelly inside. Her legs were wrapped around his thighs, and the huge bulge of his arousal was rubbing against her. She heard herself making sounds she'd never made before as he kissed her cleavage, tongued her nipples through the thin cotton fabric, and she could feel him throbbing against her cleft, half inside her even through their clothes.

Someone spoke harshly somewhere near them, a deep, male voice, and Caitlin felt Ryder's warmth move slightly back from her, leaving her dazed and wanting.

She heard her own name, and she looked past Ryder into the dark of the courtyard, too dazed to recognize him at first…and then her heart plummeted.

Jagger.

Caitlin felt a sharp jolt of dismay. She was beyond flustered. *What had he seen?* They'd been practically doing it against the tree. She slipped from the wall, but her legs were so shaky that they barely held her up; her mouth felt bruised, and inside, she was still throbbing.

Beside her, Ryder seemed completely unperturbed, even relaxed. "I believe it's the Vampire DeFarge."

Jagger took a sharp step forward and pulled Caitlin to his side. "Are you all right?" he demanded. Caitlin nodded, mortified, and saw his concern for her replaced by anger. "Do you realize you just left a crime scene?"

"You know very well if we'd stayed it would have been more trouble for you in the long run," Ryder said calmly.

Through her embarrassment, Caitlin was becoming aware that the two of them were talking like old— well, not friends, but old enemies, anyway.

"I was watching out for her," Ryder was saying.

"That's what you call watching out for her?" Jagger said murderously, glancing at the tree.

"That's the pot calling the kettle black, isn't it? I hardly have to tell you about the allure of a Keeper," Ryder shot back.

Caitlin could feel Jagger's anger flare, and her own

pulse spiked in alarm as she realized the men were a breath away from fighting.

"Jagger. *Jagger,*" she repeated sharply. "He knows about the dead man. He's a shapesh—"

"I know who he is." Jagger bit off the words, his eyes never leaving Ryder's face. "As I recall, you were run out of town on a rail."

Ryder half smiled, and despite herself Caitlin was fascinated, feeling something ancient and powerful at work. These…beings, who were to all outward appearance men in their prime, had been alive long before even her parents had been born.

"A complete misunderstanding on the part of the girl's family," Ryder answered Jagger.

Caitlin felt herself freezing up at his words. *That's right,* she told herself, pushing her feelings down hard. *Always remember he's a shifter. That's his nature. Using people and leaving them. Stay away.*

"You come back into town and people start dropping dead. That kind of coincidence doesn't sit well with me," the detective said icily.

"No coincidence at all," Ryder retorted. "We have a mutual problem, and I'm on the job." Jagger eyed him suspiciously, but Caitlin sensed a hesitation. Apparently Ryder did, too. "We might get farther by pooling information," he suggested. "Our friend on the other block wasn't the first death, was he? And the deaths are presenting as overdoses, right? You're probably thinking a bad batch of meth."

Now it was Caitlin's turn to eye Ryder suspiciously. That was exactly what Jagger had said to her. It set off alarm bells.

"It's not meth," Ryder said.

"What, then?" Jagger said, the words clipped.

"I want to see the bodies," Ryder said.

Even as they were walking through the doors of the morgue, Caitlin had no clear idea of how they'd ended up there. Saying "yes" to Ryder was the last thing she had expected Jagger to do; she could barely wrap her mind around it.

The medical examiner's office was in the Central Business District, a five-story brick building.

The halls were eerie at night, shining linoleum reflecting the blue light from the streetlights outside the windows. The vampire, the shapeshifter and the Keeper walked together through the watery light.

Caitlin was uncomfortably aware of Ryder's body beside hers; the hall wasn't narrow, but he was walking so close beside her that their arms and thighs were constantly brushing. *Getting in my space,* she thought resentfully. *Imprinting.*

The truth was, her body was still buzzing from their…"kiss" didn't even begin to cover it. She could feel him electrically beside her, and she could smell him in her hair, smell the leather of his jacket on her skin. He looked at her through the reflected blue light, and she turned to fire in the darkness, remembering his mouth hot and demanding on hers, his hands slipping over her breasts….

Jagger stopped in front of a door and unlocked it, pushing it open for Caitlin to step through. The room on the other side was chilly and uncomfortable—grim, dark, with two walls of lockers. *Meat lockers,* Caitlin thought morbidly, which, in the end, was exactly what they were.

Jagger flipped on the lights, a stark, too-white glow of fluorescence, checked a slip of paper in his hand and walked to a locker midway down the wall. He opened it and slid out the drawer. Caitlin and Ryder moved closer, and the three of them looked down at the stiff, gray-fleshed corpse.

"Victim number four. Stephen Boylan, a tourist from Biloxi. Car salesman. In town with his wife, celebrating their sixth anniversary. Dropped dead on Bourbon, October 20. Coroner ruled methamphetamine overdose."

Ryder bent over the body, all focus now. "No meth here. Normal, healthy-looking teeth, hair, skin. No scabs or sores. No malnutrition." He took the corpse's head in both hands and examined it, as well. "No irritation of nasal tissues."

"Those are indicators of long-term use. You

wouldn't necessarily see that in a first-time user," Jagger said tightly.

Ryder looked across the corpse at Jagger. "What about previous victims? Any of those indicators?"

"No," Jagger answered.

"And the chemicals in the tox screens are close but just don't add up, right?" Ryder said, his eyes steady on Jagger's face.

"No," Jagger said slowly. "They don't add up."

"What are the chances that…four?—now five?—tourists in a row decide to try crank for the first time and all end up OD'ing? Within two weeks?"

"Not good," Jagger agreed—not happily, Caitlin thought.

"And what did the coroner say about the levels of adrenaline?"

Caitlin saw Jagger stiffen.

"Wildly high," the detective admitted, his reluctance obvious. "He thought it was an anomaly."

"An anomaly that just happens to present in every single one of the victims?" Ryder asked.

Jagger was silent, and Caitlin could tell Ryder's words grated on him.

Ryder glanced at Caitlin, then back to Jagger. "We saw that last one die," he said softly. "It looked like his heart was about to explode out of his chest."

Now Jagger looked to Caitlin—for confirmation, she realized. She nodded silently.

Ryder nodded, too. "And that, right there, is your main clue. That adrenaline overdose is what happens when a walk-in leaves a body."

Chapter 7

"A walk-in," Jagger said sharply.

At the same time Caitlin demanded, "What's a walk-in?"

"Other cultures have other names for them. Devas. Dervishes. Shadow people. *Qlippoth*." Ryder's voice echoed in the chilled room. "They're disembodied beings, a formless archetypal energy that can take over human or animal bodies. It's an amorphous energy that craves human form, but once it's actually in a body, all it does is indulge its senses and wreak havoc, burning out the body so quickly that the human host dies of stroke or heart attack, just as in a massive drug overdose."

Caitlin's earlier distraction had disappeared; she was completely focused on the eeriness of what she was hearing and the gravity of the situation.

Ryder looked to Jagger. For a moment all jockeying for position was gone, and the shifter spoke colleague to colleague. "For some reason these particular entities cause a biochemical change in the human host that presents with symptoms of a meth overdose: massive adrenaline jolt, heart failure—but without quite the same resultant chemical residue. This is what you have to know. Drug and alcohol use make it easy for walk-ins to take over. They can most easily get into a human being when that person is weak or in an altered state of some sort: drunk, high, suicidal—or in the middle of sex."

He didn't look at Caitlin as he said the last, but she could feel his words sizzle through her body.

"So that makes pretty much everyone on Bourbon Street a target," Jagger was saying.

"Give the man—excuse me—give the vampire an ice-cold goblet of blood," Ryder said. Jagger gave him a lethal look but didn't rise to the bait as Ryder continued. "Bourbon Street is as enticing to a walk-in as it is to a pickpocket or any other predator. Easy prey. And the…excesses of the arena make it easy for them not to be noticed by anyone around them. Weirdness abounds."

Jagger's ascetic face was deep in thought. "What

are they doing here? Why New Orleans, suddenly?"

"They're riding the trade winds," Ryder answered. "There's a whole group of them that are linked up together by now. I've been tracking them from Africa. They blew through the Bahamas, caused some pretty bad damage over late summer and early fall. Do some research into drug-related deaths and you'll see—same pattern, spread out over various islands and jurisdictions."

Caitlin could tell from his expression that Jagger would be following up on that immediately.

Ryder continued. "These are not normally the most conscious of beings, but there's one in their midst which seems to have taken control of the herd. The others have for—whatever reason—coalesced around that one entity." Caitlin was watching his face intently and saw that he darkened as he spoke. There was something more personal there than he was admitting to; she could feel it in the weight of his voice as well as see it in his expression. Ryder glanced at her briefly, as if feeling her scrutiny, then looked back to Jagger. "They're following this one, and I think 'it' is specifically targeting New Orleans because the feeding is so good. As you said, if you're looking for drunk, stoned or humping, Bourbon Street is the place to be. Especially on—"

Caitlin felt a chill. "Halloween," she murmured,

finishing his sentence. Halloween in New Orleans was by no means the month-long party that Mardi Gras was, but as revels tended to do, it brought out all of NOLA's bacchanalian fervor.

"Three days away," she said, feeling ill.

"And every drunk, stoned tourist in town is up on Bourbon Street for the night," Jagger concluded grimly. The three of them went silent, looking down at the corpse in front of them.

"We have to move fast," Ryder summed up.

"What is this 'we,' Kemosabe?" Jagger asked him, his tone just this side of scathing.

Caitlin was jolted back to the present, surprised at his sudden vehemence.

"What the hell do you care what happens to this city?" Jagger went on.

Ryder's face closed like a shutter. "That's none of your business, vampire."

"It is if we're going to work together, shifter," Jagger replied, equally cold.

"I have a job to do," Ryder said evenly. "This city is where it led me. I have no attachment here one way or the other."

Caitlin felt as if she'd been stabbed in the heart at his words, and the feeling was frightening. *I can't trust him. He doesn't care. It's all a job for him.* She scrambled for detachment, to make herself cold. *We*

*haven't done anything but kiss. Why should I feel
torn apart?*

"And who hired you for this 'job'?" Jagger demanded.

Ryder didn't budge. "That's my business."

"Then we're done here, aren't we?" Jagger said.
The two of them faced off, stony and implacable.

Oh, good grief, Caitlin thought. *This is why
nothing ever gets done in the world. Men.*

Even if neither of the men she was now looking
at was a man at all, technically speaking.

Jagger turned on his heel to go, a move of dismissal.
But Ryder had one more trick up his sleeve.

"You're not quite done, vampire."

There was such power in his voice that Jagger
turned back. Ryder waited an infuriatingly long moment before he continued.

"I think that entity went after Cait specifically."

There was instant, electric tension in the chilled
room, a palpable blend of Jagger's disbelief and Caitlin's sudden jolt of fear.

"There was only one *entity* going after Cait, as far
as I could see," Jagger responded, his voice dripping
sarcasm.

Despite her apprehension, Caitlin felt outrage at
the men talking about her as if she weren't even there.
But before she could protest, Ryder was snapping
back at Jagger.

"Joke about it if you like," Ryder said, and his tone could have frozen water. "But once inside a body, walk-ins generally only care about their own pleasure, and the only things they notice are what's right in front of them. They resort to violence only if someone or something is standing in their way. But that possessed tourist was stalking Cait—he followed her from Bourbon."

Jagger was motionless, processing. Caitlin's stomach was roiling, remembering the force of the tourist's body barreling into her, knocking her down, the hands around her neck, choking the life from her....

Ryder's eyes were boring into Jagger's.

"So consider. If these entities want full reign of the city, and if they, or at least their leader, are aware of the Keepers, who do you think they're going to want to neutralize first?"

Even through her own emotional reaction, Caitlin admired how Ryder seemed to have read Jagger, whose Achilles' heel was Fiona. If there was anything that would keep Jagger engaged...

But in her own head, Caitlin was a million miles away already. Let the men fight it out on their own. She knew exactly what she needed to do next.

I have to talk to Danny. If we're dealing with discarnate entities, I need someone who can look into the astral and see what's really going on. If anyone can find these things...

She felt someone watching her, and looked up sharply to see Ryder looking at her, as if he could hear her thoughts. And for the first time she realized there was a good possibility that he *could* read her thoughts, or something like it. Not all shifters were psychic, but the more developed their other skills, the more likely they were to pick up on information while passing through the astral.

How psychic is he? Like Danny? If he were half, or even a quarter, as adept, he could be dangerous to her....

"All right," Jagger said, drawing Caitlin's attention back to the moment. "All right. What would you suggest we do next?"

Caitlin could tell how much it cost him to ask the question, and she had to admire his willingness to ask.

"If we can get hold of one of the walk-ins while it's in a body, before the host dies, I may be able to bind it and force it to talk. We need to track down the lead entity."

Caitlin could see Jagger's mind working. "That means patrolling Bourbon," he said, and reached into a suit coat pocket. "I need to make a phone call," he said, and Caitlin could tell by the quiet anxiety in his voice that he was thinking of Fiona. Even as he speed dialed, he was stepping outside the room for privacy.

The instant the door closed, Ryder turned on Caitlin. "What were you thinking, just then?"

"Just when?" she asked innocently, and thought in triumph, *So he* can't *read my thoughts, not precisely.*

"You know very well what I'm talking about," he said roughly, and in two steps he was towering over her, taking her by the wrists. "What are you holding back?"

She tried to jerk away from him, but he simply pulled her against him, holding her wrists behind her back, his arms encircling her waist, immobilizing her.

"This isn't a game we're playing here," he said.

"I'm not playing," she snapped at him, and tried to push him away.

"Neither am I," he said, as he continued to hold her against him, legs against legs, hips against hips.

She could feel the live heat of him, warming her body to the core, and his sheer raw power. There was no question that she would not go free until he decided to let her go, and as he stared down at her, Caitlin felt herself turning to liquid, knowing he was going to kiss her again.

Instead he released her and moved a step away— just as Jagger pushed back in through the door. He stopped in the doorway, looking at the two of them, the distance between them obviously not fooling him for an instant.

"Your sisters are fine," he told Caitlin in a clipped voice. "I'm taking you home now."

Caitlin was about to protest that she wasn't a baby, and how dare he, then realized that would only make her sound like the baby she claimed not to be, and besides, her alternative was staying with Ryder, and she didn't want to talk to him, much less…everything else that could and obviously *would* happen if they were alone together.

"Good," she said, and shot Ryder a superior look.

Jagger held the door for her, and she marched out of it. Ryder followed. In the dark hall outside, Jagger locked the door behind them, then turned to Ryder.

"I suggest we meet for breakfast, and you can fill all the Keepers in on what you know."

"I'd be delighted to meet the family," Ryder said with a straight face, but his eyes slid to Caitlin.

She felt herself tremble again, and instantly was furious with herself for even responding.

A shifter. The last person—make that nonperson— you can trust. Get a grip.

She stuck close to Jagger all the way out of the building.

Chapter 8

Caitlin was uncomfortable—squirming, actually—in the passenger seat of Jagger's unmarked Cavalier as he drove the few short miles back to the Quarter and the small compound she shared with her sisters.

His too-perfect vampire profile was chiseled, stony, beside her, and his disapproval rolled off him in waves. Still, he managed not to say anything until they were through the security gates and parked inside the compound, and he was finally walking her across the courtyard to her front door. *Vampires and their eternal manners.*

He stopped outside her door, under the shadows of magnolias. "Caitlin, we don't know each other

well yet. But I knew *that* one about a century ago."
He didn't use a name, and he didn't have to. Caitlin's
face was already burning in the shadowed dark.

"And I don't want to see you hurt. You shouldn't
trust him," he finished, earnestly.

"I don't need you to tell me that," she flared. And
then she couldn't help herself; she went on to say
something unforgivable. "You don't have to worry
about me. Keepers and Others shouldn't mix, period.
It's a conflict of interest."

She pulled open her door and flounced inside, but
not before she'd seen the startled look of pain on his
face.

She regretted it even before she'd closed the door,
and she had the impulse to pull it back open, to call
out, "I'm sorry," after him. And in fact, before she'd
even made it to the staircase she was turning around,
crossing to the door....

But when she stepped outside, she could see him
across the courtyard, in the light of the moon and
the sprinkled lights from Fiona's balcony. He and
her sister were already locked in an embrace, as if
they hadn't seen each other for years, and they were
completely oblivious to her.

Caitlin stepped back inside her doorway and
closed the door, roiling with emotion: resentment,
regret.

Then she hardened herself, locked the door behind her and stalked up the stairs to her bedroom.

After she'd shed her clothes, she stood under the steamy spray of the shower and lathered herself with lavender to get the morbid, formaldehyde smell of the morgue off her…but found her thoughts obsessively straying to Ryder and the feel of his hands on her, the unbearable pleasure of his mouth on her breasts. Her mouth and nipples felt swollen under the hot pulse of the water, and she ached between her legs, as wet inside as she was out.

She leaned back against the tile wall, imagining him stepping into the shower with her, his body hard and naked against hers in the steamy heat…and then forced herself to open her eyes, to straighten. *All right, that's enough of that.*

She shut the water off and grabbed a fluffy towel.

Minutes later, wrapped in a silk robe, she stood at the French doors of her bedroom and combed out her hair, a little more savagely than necessary, while she tried to breathe and focus.

She looked down over the quiet compound, the three-part house she and her sisters shared, and let her mind go to what could happen if a whole horde of discarnate entities intent on possessing human bodies suddenly descended on New Orleans during the revel that Halloween would be. If drugs and alcohol and sex made walking-in easier, then the walk-ins would have the easiest pickings in the world.

Ryder was right. They didn't have much time.

She turned to her dresser and looked at a silver-framed photo of her parents, arms wrapped around each other, looking at each other in the way they always looked: lovers, partners, soul mates.

"What do I do?" she whispered, not realizing she spoke aloud.

The photo was silent, but their palpable radiance brought tears to her eyes.

She brushed at her face angrily.

Danny, she thought again. *These walk-ins aren't anything we can find by looking for them in the real world. They're in the astral.*

I have to talk to Danny.

She glanced at the clock and was startled to see it was three-fifteen in the morning. Bons Temps would be closed, and God only knew where Danny and Case would have gotten themselves to—or what they'd gotten *into*.

Tomorrow, then, she thought, and then stopped, staring out through the doors, down into the court-yard.

A shadow moved under a tree.

There was someone outside.

Without thinking, Caitlin backed slowly away

from the French door, then turned and bolted for the door into the hall.

She ran down the stairs toward the front door, her bare feet silent.

At the door, she paused to draw a breath, and then she threw the door open and strode out into the courtyard.

"Who's there?" she demanded, staring out toward the tree where she'd seen someone move. She saw nothing but shapeless shadows at first, and then she caught the glow of a cigarette.

Part of the dark disengaged itself from the rest and stepped slowly forward; she caught a glimpse of a gaunt face and a familiar twisted grin.

Case.

"What the hell are you doing here?" she demanded, breathless.

"What, you aren't going to invite me in?" the musician/shifter mocked her, as he took a last drag of the cigarette and flicked it away onto the paving stones.

Caitlin was on the verge of telling him to go straight to hell when she realized that this was exactly the chance she needed.

"Of course, what was I thinking?" she tossed off. "I've been lying awake just hoping you would show up."

She was gratified to see a startled flicker cross

his face; she'd surprised him, though he covered with a lazy drawl. "Good to know things haven't changed."

She stepped back toward her patio and held the door open. He walked by her, slowing to look over her body as he passed. She realized she was in nothing but a short silk robe, bare legs, bare feet, bare... everything.

Oh, well...it can't hurt.

Before she closed the door behind him, she glanced quickly toward Fiona's wing of the house, afraid that they'd woken Jagger. *I don't need him butting in.*

But her sister's windows were dark. *They're probably otherwise engaged,* Caitlin thought with ire, and she shut the door behind her, a little harder than necessary.

Inside, Case had already made his way to the liquor cabinet; she found him pouring himself a straight whiskey. "What can I get you, *cher?*"

"I'm fine," she said, folding her arms as his eyes lingered on the open V of her robe.

"Fine as wine," he agreed lazily. "But tense." He drank deeply, smiling at her.

She felt a wave of fatigue, and something more disconcerting, too—attraction. *Get a grip. After all he put you through? How hard up are you?* Aloud she said, "It's three-thirty. What do you want, Case?"

"It's more about what you want," he said suggestively, as if he'd read her thoughts. And she knew too well that might have been exactly what he'd done. "I've decided not to deprive you."

This was all taking a turn down a road she didn't want to go down.

"Of what?" she asked, stalling. "Is this some kind of riddle?"

He circled back to the liquor cabinet for another drink. "You still want to see Danny, don't you?" he asked her casually as he poured again.

She felt a prickle of anticipation. "Yes. I do."

Case shrugged. "I don't see any reason that can't happen."

Instant paranoia. *And what's the catch?* "I appreciate that," she said slowly. To her surprise he laughed.

"Aw, now, *cher,* don't be like that. No strings—unless you want them, that is."

"Why the sudden change of heart?" she couldn't help asking.

He shrugged. "It's important to you." He circled closer. "But it would help if you told me what's so urgent."

She hesitated, but what was the harm? "Those tourists are dropping dead because they're being possessed by…entities. They're called walk-ins. They're taking over human bodies and going on rampages, and when they leave, they burn out the bodies in a way that looks like a meth overdose."

"Walk-ins," Case repeated, quirking an eyebrow. "Never heard of them."

"I hadn't, either," she admitted.

"What do you think Danny can do?" He frowned.

Now that she'd decided to tell him, she found it was a relief to be able to talk to someone familiar. "These things are completely formless. When they're not inside a body, they spend all their time in the astral. And we need to find them before—before Halloween would be good, because that's when they'll have the chance of doing the most damage."

Case looked skeptical but intrigued. "That is a wild story, *cher*. How do you know all this, anyway?"

Caitlin took a long pause, but then felt reckless. "There's a shapeshifter in town who says he's been hired to track them."

"How do you know he's not blowing smoke up your ass?"

Caitlin flinched at the language, but this was Case; she should expect it by now.

"Don't tell me you trust him," he pressed her, his ice-blue eyes probing her face.

"Hardly," Caitlin scoffed. "He's a shifter, through and through. But I think he's right about these things. I saw…" She shuddered, remembering. "I saw a man die tonight. There was something inside him, struggling to get out, and then…there wasn't. And whatever it was, when it left, it left the body fried. It was awful."

She realized she hadn't had time to process the fact that a man had died right in front of her, a grotesque, horrific, painful end to an innocent human being who had wanted nothing more than a good time in her city. She found she was shaking, tears stinging her eyes. She turned away, fumbling for the arm of the sofa to sit down.

And then Case was striding toward her, pulling her into his arms, holding her. "I'm sorry," he whispered into her hair. "I'm sorry you had to see that."

Her instinct was to pull away, but to her vast surprise, he didn't try to kiss her, didn't make any moves, just stood holding her, his arms strong and sure around her, and suddenly she felt warm and comforted and not so alone.

Case was stroking her hair, and she found feelings stirring she wasn't aware she still had. Attraction, for the first time in years. Confusing, conflicting…

As if feeling the change in her, Case tipped her head up to his and moved to kiss her, but she turned quickly, and he only caught her on the cheek.

"No," she murmured, without pulling away.

"We're alike, Caitlin. We understand each other." He kissed her mouth this time, and in spite of a warning voice in her head, she felt herself starting to respond, her body moving against his.

He was so familiar. They'd known each other for years, after all.

He'd been her teacher, her companion, her lover….

She raised her hands weakly to push him away, and he took her wrists in a strong grip and pinned them behind her back as he moved against her, opening her mouth under his.

His shoulders were so broad…and his thighs were thick, roped with muscle….

Not Case…she realized. The body against hers was not Case.

She opened her eyes and looked into his and saw not blue, but green.

And at that moment she wrested her wrists away and shoved him savagely. "No."

The air around him shimmered, shifted…and the illusion was gone. Ryder stood in front of her, his shirt half open, revealing a man's body, not a boy's.

"Liar. Cheat." She practically snarled at him, fumbling to close her robe, still panting, her heart racing with desire—and fury.

For the first time he looked flustered himself. "I'm sorry. I didn't intend… I was… I got caught up."

Ryder was mortified. He'd intended only to get information from her, taking the form of the young shifter she obviously, foolishly, trusted enough that she was willing to spill any amount of information. But then she'd started to cry, and once he had her in his arms...

She was plainly furious, flushed with anger—and desire, he noted, her skin rosy with unmistakable arousal, and that made him harden again with the desire to finish what they'd started.

He moved toward her again, and she backed away from him.

"I want you out."

"There's one false word in that sentence," he said, and caught her around the waist to kiss her roughly again, backing her against the wall and grinding himself slowly against her as he crushed her mouth under his...hearing her gasp and feeling her trembling under him, the fire racing through her body, meeting the fire in his.

Then he released her abruptly. He stared down at her where she stood flushed and shaking against the wall...felt his own heart racing....

"I think you knew that was me," he told her. "And I think you know what you want."

Then he turned and walked out of her house.

Caitlin slammed the door hard behind him. She was in a fever pitch of anger—and just plain fever. She refused to think of what he'd said to her or whether it was true. He'd used his Other skills to deceive and seduce. He was entirely in the wrong.

And yet her face burned, remembering his quiet accusation that she had known it was him making love to her...and she felt his body against hers again, his mouth crushing hers....

Stop it, she ordered herself. *He's a shifter. He tricked you. This is war.*

Chapter 9

Four sleepless hours later, Caitlin dragged herself out of the shambles of the bed she'd done nothing but toss and turn in all through the last small hours of the morning. She cursed Ryder and his entire family.

Shuffling into the bathroom, she caught a glimpse of herself in the gilt-framed mirror and groaned. She looked more hungover than the most out-of-control tourist at Mardi Gras, and she hadn't even had the pleasure of indulgence.

Oh, yes, you did, a traitorous voice whispered in the back of her head. *There was pleasure all right. Your problem is you didn't get indulged enough.*

She silenced the voice with a murderous hiss and stumbled into the shower.

Dressed, aspirined and hidden behind oversized sunglasses, Caitlin emerged from her front doorway into a sadistically glaring sun. She was hoping to slip out of the compound for coffee, but as she hurried across the paving stones of the garden, she heard Fiona's melodic voice calling down to her from the balcony.

"Caitlin!"

Caitlin groaned inwardly and turned. Fiona stood out on her balcony, blonde hair a halo of light, waving, beckoning her, then pointing down toward the first floor. Shauna was lounging against the door frame, drinking from a mega-mug of coffee.

The last thing Caitlin wanted or needed this morning was Fiona's gentle intuitiveness and Shauna's sharp eyes. But when sisters called…

She sighed and headed for Fiona's wing of the house.

Caitlin walked through Fiona's living room, following feminine voices and the smell of what was probably a cheese and sausage omelet from the kitchen, moving past antiques and eclectic art, including several large paintings of Rodrigue's Blue Dog. On one wall was a huge red brick fireplace with a pink marble mantel, and Caitlin slowed, as always, to look at the photos of their parents, and herself and her sisters as children, that lined the mantel.

It's not fair, she thought, finding herself teary. *We had so little time with them. They were only trying to do something good.*

She angrily brushed tears from behind her sunglasses and forced the thoughts away. She was so emotional today; she had to get a grip.

As she reached the kitchen, she saw Fiona at the stove, standing over, yes, an omelet pan. Shauna sat sprawled at the kitchen table in front of an artfully arranged plate of pastries and strawberries.

"Very Gaga," Shauna said, through a mouthful of beignet, waving the remainder of the pastry vaguely toward Caitlin's sunglasses. "You turning vamp on us or something? Oops, sorry, Jag, no offense," she apologized breezily.

"None taken," said the vampire, from where he leaned, long-legged, against the sink.

Great, Jagger, too. That's all I need. Caitlin reluctantly removed the sunglasses, revealing her ravaged face.

"Ooh, girl. Tie one on last night, did we?" Shauna gloated.

Fiona said nothing, but Caitlin could feel her older sister's eyes on her, probing.

"No, I didn't," she snapped. "I saw a man die last night, so I didn't sleep much."

"Oh, kiddo," Fiona said, and moved to her quickly, folding her into a hug. "I'm so sorry."

Caitlin's instinct was to pull back, but in fact her sister's embrace was so warm that Caitlin couldn't help but feel comforted, and it was Fiona who finally released her.

"Jagger's been telling us about it." Fiona glanced toward her man. "It sounds horrifying."

"Who the hell ever heard of a walk-in?" Shauna demanded, unfolding her long legs and crossing to the stove to dig into Fiona's omelet, as usual not bothering with a plate.

"Well, we need to find out as much as possible. I think Jagger's right. We need to meet with this Ryder Mallory," Fiona said.

Jagger straightened from the sink. "I'll be on my way," he said casually. "You three will want to talk it over."

He wasn't a Keeper, and he didn't belong at any powwow of theirs, but Caitlin had to admit that it was tactful of him to leave them alone. *Those damn sensitive vampires.*

Caitlin watched from the kitchen doorway as Fiona walked him to the front door, and of course he pulled her into a kiss, and of course, it was tender and lingering and everything a kiss should be....

Caitlin turned her head away and stalked over

to the kitchen counter, where she poured herself an oversize cup of coffee.

"The eggs are great," Shauna enthused, forking more into her mouth. "You should have some. You're wasting away."

Caitlin, who couldn't process a thought before coffee, much less face food, ignored her.

"So this Ryder Mallory person," Shauna continued, not missing a beat. "Is he hot or what? 'Cause a supernatural bounty hunter—that sure sounds hot."

"He's not a person," Caitlin snapped, and gulped coffee. *Oh, lifesaving.* She drank more, feeling the caffeine rush into all the deprived parts of her body. When she finally raised her head from the cup, she realized her sister was studying her speculatively.

"Wait a minute, wait a minute…is that why you look like death warmed over this mornin'? You *slept* with him?"

"Of course I didn't," Caitlin answered back, in a fury. "Would you have sex with a werewolf?" she snapped out at Shauna, before she realized that Fiona had stepped back into the doorway. Caitlin felt terrible, seeing her sister flinch, knowing she'd delivered the blow.

Well, it's how I feel, she thought. *I can't help how I feel.*

Fiona gathered herself and spoke quietly. "We need to meet with this bounty hunter. As soon as possible, I think. Jagger has had some experience with him. He's—well, Jagger says he's a shifter, with all the attendant…shifting, but he's been on the job for a long time, and the suspicious deaths are real, so we need to take what he says seriously."

"Bring it on," said Shauna, and reached for another pastry.

What that girl can eat, Caitlin thought resentfully. *She burns it off just breathing.*

She was about to tell Fiona she would rather swallow ground glass than talk to Ryder or see him ever again, and then she stopped, realizing.

If the others have a meeting, that gets Ryder and Jagger out of the way. Which means I can go talk to Case—and possibly Danny—alone.

A chill of excitement ran up her spine. *This is my chance.*

Fiona was looking at her, frowning—that infuriating intuition. As best she could, Caitlin suppressed her thoughts, envisioning a solid brick wall right behind her eyes, and a moment later Fiona looked away.

Caitlin breathed out invisibly. Aloud she said, "You're right. We need a meeting. What time is good?"

They decided on eight, Caitlin maneuvering for a time after dark, to ensure Case and Danny would actually be conscious and moving.

Fiona added, "Jagger will call if there are any incidents in the city. We should all keep all our senses open."

Caitlin was nodding and already easing for the door, when Fiona said, "And Cait…"

Caitlin stopped in her tracks. *Here it comes*, she thought wearily.

But typical Fiona—despite Caitlin's jab at Jagger, she was nothing but gracious and loving—she said "We both owe you an apology."

Shauna looked up, with a "Who, me?" look. Caitlin was also confused—she was the one who should be apologizing.

Fiona continued. "You were right from the beginning—you caught the danger before anyone did, and you did what you needed to do to figure it out."

"Oh…" Caitlin mumbled uncomfortably. "Well, that's our job, isn't it?" And then she was backing toward the door. "Look at the time. I need to get to the shop."

Fiona took a step toward her. "Are you sure you're all right?" she asked, searching Caitlin's face.

"Of course," Caitlin answered breezily. "Except for an imminent walk-in attack on the city, I'm just fine."

"We'll take care of the shop today. You need some sleep," Fiona said firmly.

Caitlin was about to protest, but a second's reflection made her realize she was dead on her feet, and she was going to need all her resources to deal with Case and Danny and whatever might unfold that night.

"That would be great," she said honestly. "Are you sure?"

"Absolutely positive," Fiona said. "You sleep."

Back in her bedroom, Caitlin pulled all the shades and curtains, and stripped to her panties and bra. At that point she could barely move her limbs, but even through the fog, as she settled back on fluffy down pillows, she was congratulating herself on her plan. Setting up a meeting was a positively brilliant way to ditch Ryder and Jagger so that she could talk to Case and Danny alone.

Thinking of Ryder was a mistake, though, especially thinking of him while she was in bed. Her body immediately started doing the same infuriating dance, betraying her with memories of his kiss bruising her mouth, his hands on her, stroking her between her legs, sucking her breasts...the thick, hard length of him pressing insistently against her...opening her... poised to plunge....

She moaned in exasperation and pushed back the blankets, then threw her bare legs out of bed and stood. She stalked to a cabinet and shoved through various glass bottles of tinctures and potions until she found what she needed: a sleeping draught. She tossed back the whole thing, dropped the bottle in the sink and went back to bed.

Ryder woke to a straining erection, with the smell of Caitlin MacDonald's perfume a teasing memory on his skin. He felt…well, besides hard, it was difficult to say what he felt. Annoyance that he'd walked out on her, when so plainly, if he'd stayed, she would have succumbed, and he could be rolling over on top of her right now to take care of his present condition. He also felt some residual guilt for having deceived her. It was a point of honor that he never seduced a woman in anything other than his true form; using his natural talents later in bed was a different story.…

And there was something else, something less tangible…not just a desire to be satisfied, but a longing…a longing that seemed to be specifically for her.

His erection stirred with the thought of her, and for a moment he luxuriated in the fantasy of plunging deep inside her, feeling her nails digging into his back, hearing her helpless sighs in his ear as he brought her to the brink.…

So why was he the one who felt helpless?

He lay against the pillows of his hotel bed, frowning…and then threw back the sheet and stalked to the bathroom. There was, after all, work to be done, and he didn't need the distraction of Caitlin MacDonald. Or anyone else, for that matter.

* * *

There was a message on his voice mail from the vampire detective, informing him that the Keepers had requested a meeting with him at eight that evening. That worked perfectly for Ryder, as he wanted to do some investigating on his own. So, dressed and showered, he headed down to Canal Street to rent a car for the day, a much more practical option than renting a car that would only gather dust in the $30 a day lot of his hotel, while he spent day after day doing what every other resident of the Quarter did to get around: walk.

Ever since he'd arrived back in town, Ryder had been thrilled to see that though rebuilding was ongoing, the French Quarter and the Garden District were as colorful, lively, eccentric and thriving as ever. But he was well aware that there were areas of the city that would never be the same.

When Hurricane Katrina and the breaking of the levees had flooded and devastated the city, Ryder had been engaged in an exorcism in West Africa, but despite that distraction, he'd felt the pain of New Orleans in his own soul, a pain that surprised him, since he didn't think of himself as attached to any one place above another.

But the images of this beautiful, unique city underwater had tormented and enraged him.

He had not yet been to the outer reaches of the

city, the condemned areas, but on this day he felt compelled. He knew that in the Ninth Ward and other storm-ravaged districts there were miles and miles of abandoned houses, damaged beyond repair, block after block of silent, deserted streets, and in his experience, those kinds of neighborhoods were magnets for the most ravenous and degraded drug users, just the kind of human prey the walk-ins would be seeking. He wanted a good long look around.

It was an eerie experience, driving his rental car into the post-apocalyptic landscape that was the lower Ninth Ward. New Orleans was so flat that he could see for miles down certain streets, but all he saw were derelict houses and scorched, weed-choked lawns. Every other block or so there was a FEMA trailer or two with signs of life, but there was an overall sense of devastation. The still-present code on the houses, the X's with dates and numbers of survivors and numbers of dead, were cryptic as the voodoo symbols called *vévés,* and somehow called to mind the emptiness that must have spread through city streets during the Black Plague. On most of the houses there was a distinct water line imprinted on the walls, higher than a man's head. If he had been on this street in the midst of the storm and subsequent flooding, he would have been driving completely underwater.

Ryder abruptly pulled over to the curb, shut off the engine and got out, shutting the door on silence.

This is High Noon, he thought, staring down the empty block. *Where's the bad guy?*

He looked both ways, debating, then started to walk, feeling the hot sun on his skin. A slight wind stirred the tall dead grass in the yards, rippling an unseen left-behind wind chime. The stillness was unnerving. Ryder's own boot steps sounded hollow on the worn asphalt.

He didn't know what he was looking for, didn't know exactly why he had stopped, only that he had to be outside, to sense whatever was around him.

Yet there was a quality in the stillness of the air that made him think that something...

He paused in the street and shifted slightly. Not into any shape in particular, but into his subtle body, the energetic, nonmaterial life force that was part of every human being, but ten times stronger than the physical body in shapeshifters, subject to change by a simple act of the mind's will. It was the subtle body that talented shapeshifters could alter to make those around them see a different form or a different person entirely. But the subtle body also registered heightened perceptions that the purely physical body could miss.

In his subtle body Ryder could see the street he was on in a whole new way. He could read each house where inhabitants had died more clearly than if he had been reading the spray-painted codes; the black and wavering energy emanating from those houses was a, well, *dead* giveaway, a residual trace of the deaths that had occurred there.

And up ahead, at a house two down from the corner, he saw something else entirely. Something not merely black and emanating, but red and angry and hostile, like a scream through the astral.

In his subtle body, Ryder froze, bracing himself against the assault of angry energy. And then he felt the unmistakable agony—and release—of the death of some sentient creature.

He shifted back into his physical form and broke into a run toward the house.

He slammed through a rickety front gate that literally flew off the hinges when he shoved it, landing on the brown, overgrown grass of the postage-stamp yard. Ryder strode up the cracked walkway to the door.

He paused outside just for a fraction of a second, allowing his senses to strain toward whatever was inside.

There was only a hollow stillness.

He kicked open the door.

Chapter 10

The contrast between the dark, dank interior of the house and the glare of the midday sun outside was momentarily blinding. Realizing his vision was useless, Ryder shifted into his subtle body again and scanned the energy of the house.

There was no more vibrating. He was standing in what was essentially a cave: musty, moldy, water damaged, probably crawling with vermin. His instinct was to get the hell out of there, but there was a presence that drew him, not alive, but...

He strode to the windows and pulled down the thick, frayed curtains, so the sun spilled in.

Ryder twisted back around to stare down at the

floor, at the crumpled body of a large young man, his body wrenched back into a hideous arc, the same grotesque misshapenness of the tourist's body last night.

With one notable difference. Claws extended from the clenched fingers of this corpse's fur-covered hands.

Ryder had just enough time to think *werewolf* before he was hit hard from behind, tackled by a force strong enough to knock him halfway across the room, into a vile and moldering couch against the wall.

Ryder gasped through the pain and shoved backward, hurling his attacker off him and whipping around with a low growl, braced to fight, to kill....

Behind him, staggering to his feet, was a tall, strong young man of around thirty, with the ragged scruff-around-the-edges look of a were.

Already rage was changing man to wolf, the hair longer and shaggier than normal, facial features coarsening as nose and jaw assumed snoutlike length, savage teeth emerging....

And *huge. An Alpha,* Ryder thought with dismay.

Recovering itself, the were half turned, crouched on its haunches to spring.

Instinctively, Ryder threw up his hands and shifted...into a woman. Not just a woman, but the first woman he could think of—in fact, the only woman he'd been able to think of since he'd met her: Caitlin MacDonald. Ryder called out, as close to Caitlin's voice as he could mimic, "Wait!"

The were dropped back onto its haunches in an almost comic double-take of shock and recognition.

Ryder had been counting on the element of surprise buying him some time, but something else had happened here. It seemed that the were *knew* Caitlin.

Already the fangs and snout were retracting, the young man's features returning to a more human cast. The strapping young alpha before him actually seemed sheepish now, shuffling in shame.

Ryder couldn't help but realize that as long as the were thought he was Caitlin, he might get some interesting information out of him.

"What the *hell?*" he demanded in a fair approximation of Caitlin's voice. "What are *you* doing here?"

The young man before Ryder was now almost completely back to human, and clearly chagrined.

"Caitlin, I—I'm sorry. Louis disappeared yesterday. Patty Lee is just about out of her mind. I followed his scent, and…"

The were suddenly turned back to the body on the floor and dropped into a crouch by the corpse's side. There was obvious agony in his posture, and Ryder felt a pang of sympathy for him. "I'm so sorry," he said, as he knew she would. His mind was racing. If this alpha were had been following the dead man, then the dead man was probably a were from the same pack.

The alpha was checking the body, and Ryder could tell he was confused by the absence of wounds. Ryder himself was bothered, but for a different reason. It was deeply disturbing to think a walk-in would possess—or even trying to possess—a were, yet the painful contortions of the body pointed to exactly that.

The young were abruptly stood, pacing in a circle that was more animal than human. "What are *you* doing here? I haven't even spoken to Shauna."

Ryder recognized the name as the third of the Keeper sisters. He realized that he would probably be discovered as an impostor at any minute.

The door slammed open behind them, and a very agile, very pissed-off young woman stormed into the house, followed by several bulky men.

The woman was strong and moved with animal fluidity. Even before she spoke, Ryder was certain he was looking at another were—several of them, in fact. *Great, a whole pack.*

The female barely glanced at Ryder-as-Caitlin; her focus was on the body on the floor. She leaped forward, faltered, looked up at the first were, then back to the body. "Oh, Louis…" she growled.

"Dead," the first were said flatly.

"How?" the female snarled, and Ryder could see her face start to change, her nose darkening and elongating, the muscles of her bare arms rippling.

"I picked up his scent on Claiborne and followed it here. The Keeper was here first." He nodded toward Ryder. "Louis was already dead."

The female whipped around to stare at Ryder. Her nostrils flared, as if she were smelling some strong scent. *Busted,* Ryder thought.

"Keeper my ass—that's a *man*."

All the weres turned on him as one now, a bristling, changing pack.

Ryder braced himself. "I didn't kill your friend. But I can explain what did—" he started before the pack lunged.

Ryder quickly shifted. Holding his Caitlin form would only weaken him in a fight in which he was already at a huge disadvantage, if not mortal peril. The supernatural strength and animal viciousness of weres was something he'd experienced before. The pack before him was perfectly capable of ripping him to shreds. As he dropped back into his own body, he spun with a ninja kick and felt his boot connect with the snout of one of the young males. The were's body went flying back. But the others were already on Ryder, snarling and foaming in a killing frenzy, teeth ripping through clothes and skin.

Ryder felt himself falling to the floor from the combined animal weight of them, and the thought of Caitlin flashed through his mind. Then he hit the ground hard, feeling teeth in his arms and thighs....

A commanding male voice rang through the dim house. "Hold off."

To Ryder's vast surprise and relief, the weres fell back, drawing away from him. And though he was bleeding from several deep gouges in his arms and legs, he was no longer being chewed.

The weres moved aside for whoever had entered the house. Ryder gritted his teeth against the searing pain in his arms and lifted himself to get a glimpse of his savior.

He found himself looking at a dignified older man with silver hair, wearing an expensively tailored suit. He had discerning powder-blue eyes and the command of a professional, but the broad chest and broader shoulders gave him away as another were, though at the moment perfectly in command of his human form.

The older man's eyes went from Ryder to the contorted corpse on the floor.

The first young male were growled, "I found the

shapeshifter with Louis's body. He hasn't been dead more than fifteen minutes."

The older man's eyes rested coldly on Ryder's face, and Ryder's heart contracted. *This isn't looking good.*

"And the shapeshifter was in the form of that Keeper, Caitlin MacDonald," the female added ominously.

The older were's face went very still, and Ryder saw a ripple of coarseness, an anger that presaged the change.

"I don't know you, shifter," the older were said softly. "What were you doing, taking on Caitlin's form? If you've hurt her…" The menace was clear in his voice.

"No," Ryder said quickly. "I know the Keeper. We're working together. There's been a string of murders and your friend—" he glanced at the corpse on the filthy floor beside him "—is likely the latest of them."

At the word "murders," the weres shifted on their feet, muttering.

"Why should we believe him?" the female demanded.

"Call the vampire. DeFarge," Ryder said, hating to have to evoke Jagger's name for help, but it was slighly better than being torn apart by wolves. "He's investigating."

The older were looked him over without smiling. "All right, shifter," he said finally. "We shall see."

Chapter 11

It was dusk.

Caitlin was disoriented to realize that she'd slept the whole day. *Just like a vampire,* she thought, a bit unnerved at the thought.

On the other hand, it meant she could cook up a hell of a sleeping draught.

And she hadn't dreamed, thank God; that had provided at least some respite from her intrusively sexual thoughts of the shapeshifter.

Don't go down that road, she warned herself, and stalked to the closet.

She stared into her wardrobe and pushed clothes aside until she found what she was looking for: a lace-up dress of shell-pink that incorporated a corsetlike bodice of intricate hooks and eyes and ribbons. Both innocent and fetishistically sexy, it was something she knew Danny would like and Case would be hard-put to resist. She didn't feel one second of guilt.

When she was showered, perfumed and laced into the dress—no small task without someone else to do the lacing—she sat down at her reading table in the alcove of the living room and unwrapped the silk from the set of cards she kept at home just for herself.

She sat unmoving in her wicker chair with its high curved back and carved swan design, and let her breathing slow and her thoughts focus, then slip away to blankness.

Then she opened her eyes, shuffled and cut the cards, and dealt one.

The Lovers.

She stared down at it in dismay, then swept it up, shuffled, and dealt again.

The Lovers.

She suppressed a wave of fury at Ryder Mallory, then gathered the deck to shuffle again, and this time she held the cards in both hands, concentrating on a single question: *"Where will I find Case and Danny?"*

She drew a card and turned it over…and this time she smiled.

The Moon.

Meaning, obviously, the Full Moon Saloon.

Caitlin walked into the packed bar with its patently obvious theme. There were moons everywhere: the lighting fixtures, the neon bar signs, shining discs on the window shades, glowing cutouts in the candleholders on the table. For a moment it struck her uneasily that the Moon card was also a clear sign of deception, deceit and danger….

But of course she knew that about the situation anyway, didn't she? No news there.

She dismissed the thought and scanned the crowd. She saw Case almost instantly; the long bar was located in a raised area of the room, with wide stairs leading up to the higher level, and Case was parked on a bar stool toward the left side.

Caitlin started across the crowded floor and was gratified to turn several male heads as she made her way, not so much needing the attention for herself but because it made Case instantly notice her.

He leaned in toward the musician type hunched on the bar stool beside him and said something—the guy grabbed his drink and stood, moved away.

As Case looked down at her, she felt her face flush, remembering the night before.

Except that wasn't him, remember? She forced the

thought of Ryder and his shapeshifting trick away, climbed the stairs and slid onto the stool beside Case.

"My lucky night," he said, with that twisted grin.

The bartender immediately stepped up, and she told him, "Jack and Coke."

Case quirked an eyebrow, and she lifted her hands. "Not playing tonight?" she asked, just to have something to say.

"I'm always playing, *cher*."

"True," she said, and felt a wave of impatience. *Why does this always have to be so hard? Why can't he just tell me where Danny is, instead of these constant games?*

The bartender set her drink in front of her, and she slid it over to Case.

"Thanks for the donation. Still looking for Danny, are we?" he said, reading her. "That hurts my feelings."

"What feelings?" she snapped, before realizing that it was probably not the best way to get him to cooperate.

But, ever unpredictable, he grinned at her.

"Good point." He picked up the drink she'd bought him and took a large swallow.

She sighed. "Come on, Case, I don't want to play. What do I have to do?"

He leaned back on his stool. "Depends. What is it you need to know so bad?"

Caitlin was about to say that she'd told him last night, but stopped herself just in time. *Good thing you didn't say anything just now, because he would have been all over that for sure.*

"Those tourists aren't dropping dead from meth. There's a band of rogue entities in town—they're called walk-ins. They're made up of disembodied energy that craves human form, but once one's actually in a body, all it does is indulge its senses and wreak havoc, and burn out the body so quickly that the human host dies of stroke or heart attack."

"Party entities," Case murmured. "My kind of Other." His sharp features were thoughtful in the flickering light from the candle on the bar. "What does Danny have to do with any of this?"

Caitlin was encouraged that at least he hadn't turned her down flat. Yet.

"These things are completely formless. They spend all their time in the astral. And you know no one's better than Danny at reading the astral."

Case was silent, sipping his drink. Caitlin forced herself to be still, to wait for whatever he would say.

Finally he spoke. "How did you come to know all this?"

Caitlin had a weird wave of déjà vu—it was the

same question Ryder had asked as Case the night before, almost as if he'd seen this conversation in the future.

Caitlin answered the same way she'd answered Ryder. "There's a shapeshifter in town who says he's been hired to track them."

Case's eyes narrowed in the dark. "So that's Mallory's excuse for being in town," Case muttered, and Caitlin felt an electric thrill.

So he does know Ryder, and *he knows he's here.*

"That's no one you should be trusting, *cher,*" Case added, and it was all Caitlin could do not to roll her eyes.

How many people do I need to hear that *from?*

"I don't," she said, vehemently enough that Case flinched slightly. "But something's going on, for sure. That's why I want to talk to Danny."

Case regarded her with shifter eyes, then drained his drink and stood. "All right, then. Let's go." Dazed that it was going to be this easy, but not about to argue, Caitlin slipped off her stool and followed.

It was a beautiful night for a walk, the almost-full moon—there was the moon again—stark and white in the sky, and the air was warm, with only the slightest whisper of wind. They walked, of course; there was really nothing in the Quarter that it wasn't easier to walk to than drive. Case didn't tell her where they were going and Caitlin knew better than to ask; he'd only taunt her and not tell her anyway.

They headed straight down Chartres— "Charters," as the locals pronounced it—past shopkeepers lounging on the stoops of their stores, Case smoking and nodding to just about everyone. It was home for him, for her, and when he threw his cigarette away and reached to take her hand, she let him. *And why not?* She felt comfortable with him, nothing like the confusion she felt with Ryder, who was only in town for a job, after all—he hadn't been in NOLA for…what? A hundred years, give or take? If she was doomed to be with a shapeshifter, at least she could find one who was actually in town more than once every hundred years, couldn't she?

Case glanced at her, as if suspicious that she was being so compliant. "What is this really about? What are you up to, *cher*?"

She sighed. "We're alike, Case. You've said it before. We understand each other. Maybe there's nothing so wrong with that."

He nodded thoughtfully and tightened his grip on her hand.

They turned down the next street—Dumaine—and Caitlin thought, *I should have known.* Dumaine was the most overtly magical street in the Quarter, at least if you were going by square shop footage. There were voodoo shops and witch shops and vampire/ghost/

cemetery tour shops, and even one that veered toward the Satanic.

Case stopped in front of one of the witchcraft shops, The Occultist, and opened the door for her with mock-gallantry. Caitlin shook her head at his sudden chivalry and stepped past him into the shop. She'd been there before, of course. It catered a little too much to the dark side for her own taste, starting with the blatant pentagram and messages painted on the sidewalk outside, but it was popular with the teenagers and pagans.

The outer shop was small, holding mostly books and wands and jewelry; it did its real business in the back rooms, where readings and séances could be had for the right price.

Case put a hand on her back and walked her through the shelves, past a few tattooed patrons in black clothes and dyed black hair, past the counter where he nodded to the pierced and studded black-clad clerk falling asleep on his stool at the register, and lifted the back black velvet curtain to allow Caitlin into the back of the shop.

She felt a shiver as she stepped into the narrow, candlelit hall, a frisson of unease and anticipation. There were several shadowy doors leading off it; she could hear several people chanting behind the first. She had a weird sense of being in an old-time brothel, only a psychic one. Step right up and pay for your pleasure. And in New Orleans, who was to say that this hadn't been a real brothel at some point? Sex and the supernatural so often crossed; it often felt like the same energy was at the heart of both.

Case had moved down the hall and opened the last door, and now he was standing there waiting for her. Caitlin moved toward him, stepped past him into the room.

The long, rectangular room was black—painted-black ceiling, black floors and black candles in standing candelabra provided the only light. As Caitlin's eyes adjusted to the dancing flames, she saw that the room was dominated by an oval table in the center of the floor, on which were placed a bell, book and candle, ancient accoutrements of the séance.

There was a sagging couch at the far end of the room, and on it was a body that could have been a vampire, so still it was and so pale the face, and with long, shimmering dark hair….

Danny. Asleep or dead…but strangely angelic in the candlelight.

At that moment Caitlin's heart broke for the innocence in him.

And then she felt fury. Her brothel image had been correct. Case was pimping Danny out, selling his extraordinary gifts to any bidder.

She turned on Case, and her rage must have been

evident, or he was reading her, because he caught her wrist before she even knew she had raised her hand.

"He makes his own choices, *cher*. Do you really think he doesn't?"

"I think *you* push him down the hole," she said, trying to pull her arm away.

But he held her hard, blue eyes gleaming.

"And don't you want the same thing from him now as everyone else?"

Caitlin felt a rush of confusion—and guilt....

And then a soft, dreamy voice came from the dark at the other end of the room. "Is that Cait?"

Both she and Case stopped their fighting, like parents interrupted by a waking child. Danny was sitting up on the couch, looking still half asleep.

Caitlin pulled her arm out of Case's grasp and moved toward Danny. He reached his arms up to her, and she stooped to hug and kiss him, feeling an ache in her heart. The baby-roundness of his face was deceptive; he was so thin she could feel his bones through his clothes.

"You haven't been to see us in a while," he complained, and she wondered if he thought they were at his and Case's apartment—or crib, as they called it—which in her opinion was truer than they probably meant it to be.

"I've been—" she started, and then didn't know how to complete the sentence. *I've been...what? I've been too much of a wreck since Case dumped me to stand seeing you? It took me forever to just be able to listen to music again, even in the most casual way? I didn't want to see anyone because I screwed up so badly when my sisters needed me the most? I don't want to see you destroying yourself?*

He seemed to hear her and hugged her harder. "It doesn't matter," he said, and he might have meant it didn't matter that she'd been away, but she thought it meant that none of the other things mattered, they were unimportant.

Then he released her and pulled back. "So you're here about the creepy crawlies."

Caitlin was startled. "You know about them?"

He smiled with a blank and distant look, made more ominous by the play of candlelight on his features. "They're hard to miss. Bad intentions reek out there…."

He meant in the astral.

"What…do they look like?" she asked. Impossible question, she knew. What Danny saw was some vision of his own. But curiosity overwhelmed her.

"Bad," he said simply. "Nothingness." Something played across his face, and he withdrew even deeper into himself. "And hungry," he said tonelessly. "Endlessly hungry."

Caitlin felt a chill. The candles flickered.

With visible effort, Danny focused back on her.

"So you want me to go out there and look and see what they're up to."

Caitlin felt a sharp stab of guilt about using him and was almost ready to forget the whole thing right there. "I don't want you to do anything you don't want to do," she said.

He smiled that sweet, distant smile and said, "I want to help."

Case moved impatiently in the dark behind them. "If you two are finished with the love fest, we could actually try to get on with things."

Danny nodded.

"What do you need, bro?" Case asked.

"Move the table aside," Danny said.

Case looked at Caitlin, and she went to join him in moving the long oval table to the front of the room, against the wall and out of the way. Caitlin turned back to the center of the room just in time to see Case throwing back the rug to reveal a pentagram painted in gleaming white on the black floor, about six feet in diameter and inscribed in a circle.

Danny moved two chairs into the circle, then grabbed a third and placed it to form a triangle within the five points of the star.

"Sit," he said. Not a command, but compelling nonetheless.

With a glance at each other, Caitlin and Case took their seats within the circle.

Danny crossed to the candelabra and took candles from them one by one, cupping his hand to protect the flame as he placed one lit candle at each point of the star.

Caitlin felt a dark thrill of excitement. Danny had read for her before, and she'd observed him reading for others, but she'd never been with him for an actual séance. She had the eerie sense of something momentous about to happen.

Danny looked at her with that dreamy, not-quite-there look. "There is danger here, Caitlin. You will be vulnerable in the astral. Your life force is strong, as is your psychic force, and your Keeper powers will draw spirits of all kinds."

Caitlin swallowed. "I'll be fine." A hollow and stupid claim, she knew; there were no guarantees in the astral.

Case spoke up, roughly. "Sister Goldenhair is tough. I'll be looking out for her. Let's get this show on the road." He reached into the inner pocket of his leather jacket…and Caitlin's eyes widened as he drew out a crack pipe.

"Ready for liftoff? He smiled at her, a slow, dangerous smile.

Chapter 12

It was twenty after nine, and no sign of Caitlin.

Ryder prowled restlessly in the great room of the main house, part of the common area that the sisters shared.

The dignified elder were, whom Ryder now knew as August Gaudin, had himself delivered Ryder to the Keepers' private compound. Jagger DeFarge had arrived almost immediately after, and Ryder was left in the main room while the two Keepers, the detective and the were retired to some inner room, presumably to discuss him.

There was much to admire about the MacDonald sisters' tastes; the large room Ryder had been left in managed to be homey and sensual and magical all at once, a fitting house for the sisters' ancestral profession. The walls and bookshelves showcased mystical objects from all over the world: goddess figures, green men, filigreed mirrors, symbolic fetishes, intricate mythological tapestries. The candles were fragrant, herbal as well as floral, and Ryder noticed that the colors had been specifically chosen for intellectual focus and spiritual protection.

And the sisters themselves, Fiona and Shauna, were jewels: gorgeous, gracious, powerful beyond ordinary mortal women, both in spiritual radiance and sensual personal charm. Women he would have been irresistibly drawn to in any other situation. Instead he found himself thinking obsessively of the one absent sister, finding his very body missing Caitlin with a hunger that both startled and concerned him.

Every minute that passed was making Ryder more anxious, not for himself, but for Caitlin.

He stopped his restless pacing in front of a full-length oil portrait of an attractive couple—the sisters' parents, no doubt. The woman's beauty was a prototype for the three Keepers. August Gaudin had said enough on their drive over that Ryder understood that the werewolf had acted as godfather and protector to the young Keepers after the deaths of their parents, whom Ryder was startled to hear had sacrificed their own lives to avert full-blown war among the Others just ten years ago. Which meant that the sisters had taken over the responsibility of three hostile communities of supernatural beings when they were not only just teenagers, but teenagers trying to recover from a terrible tragedy. Ryder couldn't help but feel admiration, an uncomfortable feeling to consider on top of other more urgent feelings he had for Caitlin.

The thought of her made him frown and look toward the back hall where his hosts/captors had disappeared. He glanced again at the clock on the mantel.

It had been too long.

He had a good idea of where she would have gone; his deception of the night before had netted him the information that she would seek out the younger musician, Danny, whom Ryder gathered was a gifted psychic, as some shapeshifters were. But he'd already called the club where he'd seen Caitlin with the shifter-musicians, and neither of them was playing that evening, nor did Caitlin respond to his page.

He turned from the portrait as the Keepers, Jagger and Gaudin reentered the room.

Jagger glanced at him briefly. "I take it you think the death of the were was the work of one of these entities."

Ryder knew that Jagger had not yet examined the body; he'd gathered that Gaudin and the other weres had no intention of involving the police in any official way.

"I think you'll see for yourself," he answered the vampire.

"Do walk-ins often inhabit werewolves?" Shauna demanded.

Ryder had to suppress a smile at the youngest Keeper's blunt manner. "I've never seen it before," he told her. "Walk-ins go for humans, and weak humans at that, those whose defenses are lowered by alcohol or drugs."

"Yet you believe that Louis was killed by one of these…entities," Gaudin said.

"The were-body might process the intrusion differently, but an autopsy should reveal enough similarities to the human deaths." Except that the vampire and the others undoubtedly had no intention of subjecting the werewolf to an official autopsy, either.

"We're about to find out," Jagger said, his gaunt face set.

Ryder glanced from the men to the Keepers. "How do you manage that?"

It was a perennial problem for the Others to maintain at least one skilled doctor from each of the communities who understood the particular…needs of each species that would not have been addressed in a "Human Anatomy" class, but an autopsy was something else again.

Gaudin answered him. "The were-doctor will perform the autopsy behind closed doors. He's been trained."

Ryder noticed that Fiona had not said a word since the quartet had come back into the room; she had been checking her watch with increasing distress.

"Excuse me," she said abruptly, and moved toward the kitchen.

Ryder watched her go. Though the younger sister, Shauna, remained jaunty and upbeat, Ryder could tell from the elder sister that something was seriously off. And he didn't trust Caitlin not to have done something impetuous and dangerous.

He had been wrong, completely in the wrong, to deceive her the night before. He knew she had every right to be angry, and worse, that she might have responded to his violation of her trust by going off on her own.

But justified as her reaction might be, she would be putting herself in inconceivable danger. The walk-ins were looking for her, hungering for her power.

If she was out there in the night, he had to find her. The thought became a need, and the need became urgent.

He stuck a hand in his jacket pocket and thumbed his phone so that it rang, pulled it from his pocket and pretended to check the number, then smiled distantly toward the table where Jagger and Shauna were locked in intense discussion of the dead werewolf's last known whereabouts, and Gaudin was pacing while speaking into a cell phone, presumably with the were-doctor.

Ryder stepped into the hall as if for privacy and made a quick phone call himself.

Then he walked noiselessly toward the kitchen and looked in through the doorway to see the elder Keeper standing at the sink biting a nail as she stared out the window into the courtyard.

Fiona turned as soon as he stepped into the doorway, and he could see the effort in her smile as she said, "I'm so sorry. It's not like Cait to—"

"We have to find her." He cut her off, too impatient to bother being polite. "I don't want to alarm you, but as worried as you are, you need to be more worried."

Fiona looked at him, startled, instantly alert. "Do you know where she is?"

"Do you know a shapeshifter named Danny?"

Fiona raised an eyebrow. "The keyboard player? He and Cait used to be friends. I don't think she's seen much of him since…" Her face shadowed. "Well, there were drug issues."

There's a shock, Ryder thought cynically. Aloud he asked, "Do you know where to find him?"

"He plays at a club on Bourbon called—"

Again Ryder cut her off. "I've called Bons Temps.

Their band isn't on tonight. The one he's in with that other shifter."

"Case," Fiona said, and her tone was layered, ambivalent.

"Right," Ryder said, responding more to her tone than to the name. "Exactly."

"But what does she want with them?"

"I believe she has some idea that this Danny will be able to help her locate the walk-ins."

"Cait would never go off on her own like that, not before we even had a meeting about it," Fiona protested.

Ryder smiled thinly. "Are we talking about the same Caitlin? It seems to me that's exactly what she would do."

Fiona opened her mouth to protest, and for a moment Ryder got the idea that the Irish temper really did run in the family. And then she closed her mouth and studied him. "You're an interesting man, Ryder Mallory," she said.

"Your sister would say I'm not a man at all," he said, without cracking a smile.

"My sister has a lot to learn about men," Fiona said dryly. Again that speculative look. "And you might be the man to teach her. But if you hurt her, you'll be answering to me, shapeshifter."

There was primal power in her words, and Ryder

felt it to his core. He met her eyes. "Understood, Keeper."

They regarded each other silently, then Ryder said, "Now, where do I find these shifter friends of hers?"

"You mean we," Fiona said, her eyes blue fire.

"I mean me," Ryder said.

Chapter 13

In the dark cave of the séance room, Caitlin stared at Case from her chair in the candlelit pentacle, alarmed by the crack pipe in his hand. "No," she said automatically.

"It's how it's done," Case said jauntily. "How else do you think you're going to get into the astral, little sister?"

Caitlin knew that using drugs of any kind was acutely dangerous in a summoning or a séance. Though no doubt it opened doors, it also weakened spiritual boundaries, and opened the participants up to any number of negative forces and entities.

"Negative entities are exactly what we're after,

cher," Case said, reading her mind in that infuriating way he had. "We're not going to summon them with warm milk and sugar cookies."

Caitlin could see the logic in that, but she still felt a strong pull of warning. Case obviously considered the matter closed; he took a square of foil and a small vial from his inside jacket pocket and shook a white rock out into the foil, preparing the pipe.

Caitlin turned to Danny, hoping for backup. Instead, he reached for the crack pipe without looking at her; his eyes already had that glazed anticipation that she so hated to see, the greediness of the addiction, like an animal inside him. Case flicked his lighter and bent to light the pipe, the bow formal, a ritual in itself.

The smoke from the pipe was billowy, white, enticing. Danny sucked at it and immediately dropped his head back onto the chair, sinking into a dreamy trance. Case reached across the pentagram and took the pipe from him. He turned to Caitlin.

"Well, Keeper? Coming with us or not?"

She stared at the pipe, roiling with emotion. Part of her felt reckless, out for revenge—and desperate to prove herself. Another part was screaming a warning.

"I'll make it easy for you, *cher,*" Case offered, and stood, holding the pipe. He took two steps to stand in front of Caitlin's chair, and, looking down at her, he fired his lighter, touched the flame to the bowl. White smoke curled sensuously from the pipe. Case inhaled the smoke…and then suddenly bent over Caitlin as if to kiss her. She realized he meant to blow smoke into her mouth, blow the drug into her lungs.

And then suddenly Danny's eyes flew open and his body jerked up straight.

"Someone here. Someone else…" he croaked. His eyes were black pools, pupils dilated to the edge of the iris.

Case spun, searching the shadows. "Where?"

Caitlin's heart was pounding, every sense on alert. *Is this part of the séance? Or a real intruder?* She could see nothing human in the wildly wavering candlelight.

Case spun, and Caitlin could see the gleam of metal in his hand. A knife. "Show yourself," he hissed into the dark.

Caitlin called on her own senses. She suddenly felt someone, too. There were only the three of them in the room, so the intruder must be spirit. She felt tremendous power and anger. But there was also something about the feeling she had that wasn't threatening. Something familiar. She suddenly spoke aloud, repeating Case's command. "Show yourself." And something inside her made her add, without realizing she was going to, "I know you, shifter."

She saw a spider glowing on the wall, and then the glow grew larger and materialized…into a man.

Ryder.

Before she could even register his form, Case was leaping toward him with the knife. Caitlin shouted, *"No!"* and lunged between them. She felt a sting and wetness, and an arm seizing her, pulling her back, and somehow it was now Ryder between her and Case, and his face was a mask of fury, and she thought through dizziness that he was about to kill Case. Then the fury dissolved into alarm, and suddenly she was being scooped up, as Ryder took her out of the circle and set her down on the couch. Caitlin realized blood was pouring down her arm; she'd been cut.

"She's hurt!" Ryder raged at Case, pulling off his jacket and pressing it hard against Caitlin's arm, with his other arm wrapped around her back, holding her up against him. She could feel his heart beating wildly, charged with adrenaline.

Behind him, she could see Case pacing sullenly. "And whose fault is that? You're the intruder here, bounty hunter. Nothing would have happened if you hadn't interfered."

"Don't fight," Caitlin said, feeling light-headed, about to pass out. "Just shut up."

"What are you doing here with these clowns?" Ryder demanded.

"Hey," Case growled.

"What is that? Crack?" Ryder continued inexorably, as if Case wasn't there. "Do you know what happens when you enter the astral in an altered state?"

"Entering the astral *is* alteration," Danny said from the circle.

Ryder turned to look at him, without letting up the pressure on Caitlin's arm.

"You put her in danger," he said, his face like stone.

"It's always dangerous," Danny said. "Cait knows." He looked unblinkingly at Ryder, his eyes dilated with the drug. "If you want to do the seeing, we should do it now. There's been blood spilled in the circle. It will strengthen the calling."

"He's right," said Caitlin and Case simultaneously.

"No seance when you're high," Ryder said.

Danny smiled strangely. "I'm never not high." The smile disappeared. "Don't tell me how to do the work. She came for *me*. If you could do it, you would have done it."

Caitlin pulled away from Ryder's arm, lifted his hand so she could look at the cut. "I'm fine. Barely bleeding. Ryder..." She looked at him beseechingly. "It's our best chance...."

"I don't like it," he growled softly.

"I know," she said, and deliberately let herself lean

into him so that her breath brushed his ear. "But it really is our best chance. Please."

She felt his breath and his pulse quicken. He pulled back with an effort and looked at her. "I don't like it," he repeated, but she knew she had won.

They reassembled in the circle, four of them now.

Ryder seemed huge across from the other two, a hulking, disapproving presence.

"Keep your place, bounty hunter," Case said.

"Don't test me," Ryder shot back.

Danny's voice silenced them both. "Goddess Moon, Divine Nyx, we step into your darkness. Take me, Sister Moon. Papa Legba, let me pass. Mistress Hecate, walk with me through the crossroads…."

Caitlin found herself holding her breath, unable to move. The air in the room was shifting, rearranging; there was a cold front, and then a breath of wind, like a door literally opening in the middle of their circle. Danny straightened, his spine lengthening as if he were rising from his chair…and then his body dropped limply back against the seat, as if he'd passed out, but it felt as if something was gone from him.

Beside her, at the next point of the star, Ryder looked as riveted as she felt.

Then Danny suddenly sat up again, but abruptly,

not a human movement, but the jerky motion of a marionette.

"Who seeks counsel?" The croaking voice that came from his mouth was not Danny, was not anyone Caitlin had ever heard before. She felt a chill in the darkness.

"I see you there, children, standing beyond this portal," the voice continued, rasping, sly. "You seek me and have no questions? Or perhaps you seek to entrap?"

Ryder suddenly sprang up with an incoherent growl, knocking his chair over with the violence of the movement, and Caitlin gasped to see his face: it was a mask of rage, and his whole body was taut with fury. He started toward Danny, and Caitlin was suddenly certain he was going to attack him, kill him.

"What the hell?" Case said, alarmed.

"Ryder, no!" Caitlin cried out.

At the sound of her voice, Ryder halted. She could see him struggling to get hold of himself. And then he planted his feet and held his arms out. *"Phasmatis obscurum, ego redimio vos ut is vas. Subsisto insquequo ego impero vos progredior!"*

Caitlin recognized the Latin; it was a binding spell, to keep a spirit in a body.

Danny writhed in his chair as if some great serpent had invaded his body. Caitlin gasped out. It was the same uncontainable movement she had seen in the tourist before he died.

"No!" she cried out in sudden fear. "Get it out of him!"

"Wait…one…minute," Ryder gasped. His body strained, struggling against nothingness, and it seemed as if he was somehow holding the spirit bodily, though in fact he held nothing.

"Ask, then," Case said, in the dark. Caitlin could feel his agitation. "Be quick about it."

"Where are you?" Ryder demanded of Danny.

"I have many hosts." The thing spoke from inside Danny's body, a voice that snarled and purred at the same time, an alien sound. Danny's features were distorted, reptilian, his body lashing like a cat's tail.

"Where are you now?" Ryder pressed.

"This lovely city." Not-Danny spoke with snakelike sibilance.

"What do you want?" Ryder ground out, as if in intense pain.

"The body. The body. The human life."

Caitlin flinched at the lascivious pleasure in the creature's voice.

"Where are you now?" Ryder asked again.

"In the body," the creature taunted.

"The truth!" Ryder roared.

The thing inside Danny thrashed and coiled like a captive snake, and Caitlin realized Ryder's spell was working; the spirit was effectively bound, compelled to obedience. "This body, that body…" It sounded angry, but it answered nonetheless. Danny's eyes, flat and dead, slid to Caitlin, and crawled over her, suddenly sly again. "*That* body will do…. Yes, that will do well…."

Caitlin felt a wave of revulsion and sensed Ryder drawing near to her.

"Never," he ground out.

"Never?" the thing inside Danny taunted him. "More are coming. More will come. Some are prevented, but the door is opening, and many can pass."

"What door?" Caitlin asked, unable to help herself.

Danny's body suddenly seized and contorted, a backbend that looked both boneless and hideously painful.

"Enough!" Case shouted. "Get it out of him!"

"No," Ryder said, his eyes fixed on the young shapeshifter's body. "We've got it trapped. I can banish it—do an exorcism."

The thing in the chair lashed again, with an angry hiss.

Case turned on Ryder, his face savage. "And kill Danny—that's what you're saying. No way. Undo the binding spell *now*."

Danny spasmed again, that impossible backward

arch. He was mewling now, a hideous, animal sound.

"Ryder, please!" Caitlin cried. "He'll die!"

Ryder shot a look at her, torn, tormented.... Then he turned to face Danny's body as it roiled in the chair and launched back into Latin. "*Sis modo dissolutum exposco, validum scutum! Diutius nec defende a manibus arcam, intende!*" he shouted.

Danny's body arched and contorted again, and then he collapsed back into the chair. This time, though, his body didn't look vacant; he was recognizably human again as he breathed rapidly and shallowly. Simultaneously Caitlin and Case leaped to his side. Case pulled a phial from his coat pocket, uncorked it and waved the small bottle under Danny's nostrils. The three of them hovered over him, watching, suspended in waiting.

Then Danny's head jerked up and away from the phial, and he gasped in a huge lungful of air, a painful but human sound. Caitlin felt weak with relief.

"Okay, man. You're okay," Case muttered. Danny rose abruptly from the chair, swayed...

"Easy," Case said, and slung an arm around Danny's waist to guide him to the sofa, where he collapsed again, still breathing shallowly.

Caitlin couldn't help but see the frustration and disappointment on Ryder's face, and felt a wave of unease that the entity was loose again, out there in the astral somewhere, and now full of rage on top of that. *But Danny could have died,* she argued with herself. Her hands were trembling…no, her whole body, shaking with adrenaline.

She looked around the room for water or anything else to drink. Not seeing anything, she bolted for the door, slamming into the inner hallway, where she found a small bathroom and a water cooler. She filled several paper cups and walked quickly and awkwardly down the hall, juggling them, and slipped back into the room.

Ryder and Case were standing over Danny on the couch, arguing.

"You got what you wanted. Leave him the hell alone."

"I need to talk to him while it's fresh in—"

Caitlin pushed past both of them and crouched in front of the couch to give Danny the water she'd brought. He clutched at the first cup and drank gratefully.

"Easy," she started, but too late; he was already gagging.

Ryder turned from Case, looking disgusted. "I need to talk to him," he said to Caitlin curtly.

"Ryder," Caitlin began, but Danny interrupted her.

"Then talk, bounty hunter."

The older man looked down on the younger,

whose face was as pale as a ghost's in the darkness of the room.

"Where did you find that entity?"

Danny smiled without humor. "The astral is not a *where*."

"It was in you, and you have *no* sense of where it came from?" Ryder snapped, disbelieving.

"Did you come to learn or not?" Danny asked.

Caitlin could feel Ryder seething and held her breath as the two of them locked eyes. This constant male jockeying for power was exhausting.

"The entity has found a host," Danny said, finally.

Caitlin saw the shocked look on Ryder's face. "That's not how they work," he said brusquely. "Walk-ins burn out human bodies within a day."

"This one is evolving. It's able to contain itself, to metabolize the body more slowly."

"So it's maintaining one host?" Ryder demanded.

"That's what I said," Danny said.

"Who?"

"I didn't see," Danny answered obliquely. "The entity moves. It leaves its host in suspended animation while it wanders at will." Danny paused, drank more water—this time without gagging. "But it intends to stay. The feeding is so, so good. Irresistible."

It was basically the same thing Ryder had said

earlier, but the sly way Danny spoke made the words chilling. Caitlin shuddered.

Ryder paced, glanced at Case. "The door is opening," he muttered. Caitlin recognized the phrase; it was what the entity had said.

"I heard it." Case spoke up from where he stood in a corner of the room, and Caitlin realized that as antagonistic as his tone sounded, the two of them were communicating. "And yes, it's started."

"What's started?" Caitlin demanded.

"Samhain. The door is opening," Danny said, and the three shapeshifters looked at each other in silent agreement.

Caitlin scrambled to comprehend. Samhain was the pagan word for Halloween, one of the holiest of holidays in the pagan calendar.

Case looked at her, and for a moment it felt as it had when he was teaching her shapeshifting ways. "At Samhain the veil between the spirit world and the ordinary world is the thinnest…." Caitlin knew that, had known that for quite a while. But she was still struggling to understand what the other three apparently already knew.

Ryder told her, "You can feel the change happening, days before. It's already started. The veil lifts. The door opens. It's the easiest time of year to shift."

Case stared at Ryder. "That's why the urgency. Halloween. Massive party. People will be even drunker than usual, and no one's gonna notice if people are out of control. And then the door opens… It's Bourbon Street squared."

Ryder nodded acknowledgment at him. "We're looking at the possibility of a horde of virtual zombies on Halloween."

All four of them were silent in the dark room, contemplating the scenario.

Then Case's face closed and he shrugged. "No skin off my ass, dude. Just a bunch of tourists anyway. Who gives a shit if a few more of them drop dead?"

In the candlelight Caitlin saw anger on Ryder's face, quickly neutralized. "No, not your problem. On the other hand, you've got a pretty cushy deal in this city. No one looks too hard at anomalies like people turning into other people and things they're not. Anything out of bounds, you've got that vampire in the police department and the Keepers here—" he glanced at Caitlin "—keeping on top of things, solving problems under the radar."

Caitlin felt warm from the praise and the fact that he'd actually noticed.

Ryder turned from her back to Case, and his features hardened. "But if dozens or hundreds of people drop dead over Halloween? You're talking nationwide—worldwide—attention. You really want to see the Quarter end up a massive crime scene on national television?"

Caitlin knew exactly what he was getting at. After Katrina, the Others had had to lie low for over a year, some even leaving town, because of the massive influx of law enforcement and journalists.

Case's face was dark, no doubt as he envisioned the same scenario. "It would suck," he acknowledged belligerently. "I'm still not seeing how it's my problem."

Ryder shrugged. "It's not your problem. But if you're looking to save yourself some inconvenience, you and your friend there..." He glanced at Danny, who had fallen asleep like Alice's dormouse. "You might want to be on the lookout for where these things might be. If Sleeping Beauty gets any more hits, you could let me know."

"And me," Caitlin said quickly.

Ryder glanced at her, then back to Case. "They're going to be after the Keepers, you know. There's already been an attack on Caitlin."

Something flickered on Case's features. Caitlin knew him too well to think it was concern, but it was still...something. He turned to her. "Told you you shouldn't be wandering around in the dark, little sister. Never know what's gonna reach out and grab you."

He said the last while deliberately eyeing Ryder.

"I'm fine," Caitlin muttered.

"You can brush it off if you want to, but your sisters are in danger, too," Ryder said to her, and even as the adrenaline spiked her pulse, she admired the fact that he knew exactly what buttons to push to make *her* react, too.

Now he turned to Case again. "And the whole city's up a creek if the Keepers get taken out."

Case shrugged, the picture of nonchalance. "We can keep an eye out—why not? No skin off my ass. Now, if you don't mind, Danny should rest."

Ryder stepped forward and handed him a business card that seemed to have materialized from nowhere. Case took it, and the two men eyed each other.

Then Ryder turned and opened the door for Caitlin, waiting for her.

She looked toward Case. He made a courtly, mocking gesture. "Thanks for stopping by, little sister. Hope you got what you were looking for." Again he slid a knowing look at Ryder, which made Caitlin's face burn.

Ryder was still waiting by the door. She hesitated… then stalked out.

Chapter 14

Ryder followed Caitlin out through the dark corridor, past the bookshelves of the pagan shop. The sleepy-or-stoned clerk barely turned his head as they walked by.

Outside on the sidewalk, in the balmy night air, Ryder reached for Caitlin's arm. "I'll take you home."

"I'll be fi—" she started.

"There's an entire swarm of malevolent entities out here looking for you, and you think you'll be fine," he said, shaking his head. "There's an outer limit to independence, and you're it."

She opened her mouth again, and he put his fingers

on her lips. Just that mere touch flooded her with fire, and she was as speechless as if he'd bewitched her.

"This isn't a discussion," he said. "I'm taking you home."

Slowly he withdrew his hand, and she turned numbly to start walking down to Royal.

He fell into step beside her, but thankfully didn't touch her; her heart was already racing. The cobblestone walks were lit by electric lamplight, and their footsteps echoed against the walls of the shops.

Ryder spoke quietly. "You should call your sisters, let them know you're all right."

She looked at him, startled; it was the last thing she would have expected him to say. She was about to protest, but he cut her off.

"If you don't, I will. I had a hell of a time persuading Fiona to let me go after you alone, and I owe her that."

She narrowed her eyes, then stopped under one of the electric lamps and pulled out her cell phone. She wasn't about to talk to anyone, though; instead she texted Fiona, using a code phrase the sisters had set up to let Fiona know it really was her texting, and left a message that she was all right and headed home. She clicked off the phone irritably.

"Satisfied?" Then she realized that was entirely the wrong word to use.

His smile curved, slow and sensual. He said nothing, but he didn't have to—the look he gave her was pure, slow, searing heat.

She started walking again, shakily, but her heart was pounding now, and other parts of her were throbbing, too. And of course the Quarter wasn't helping. It was a sublimely perfect night, warm as bathwater, and perfumed, too, lilac and lavender and sugar candles and gardenia, the soft colored lights from the closed shops, music floating down from Bourbon Street, and a soft, enticing wind.

They walked for a while in silence, passing a drunk couple dreamily entwined, a group of laughing young men crossing the street in every direction but straight. But when she started to turn on Royal, she felt Ryder touch her waist, which sent another shock wave of sensation through her.

"This way," Ryder said beside her. He nodded his head down Dumaine Street, toward the river.

Caitlin hesitated.

"I just want to take a look...feel the wind," he said.

It could have been a ploy, but Caitlin knew what he meant. It was in the wind that she could always feel things, too. She fell into step beside him, and they started toward Jackson Square, the looming shadows of trees behind the iron bars.

"That was an unbelievably stupid thing you did, you know that," he said without looking at her.

Caitlin knew what he was talking about, and who, and why, but she stayed stubbornly silent.

"Those two will drag you down into the dark so fast you won't know what hit you."

"No one has to tell me," she retorted. "They're shifters, aren't they?"

He flinched, and she was meanly glad to see the dig had hit its mark.

They crossed Poydras Street toward Café Du Monde, lit up like an Edward Hopper painting against the dark backdrop of the embankment. A saxophonist was playing outside the café patio, and Ryder dropped money in his instrument case as they passed. Then they walked up the stairs to the Moonwalk.

As soon as they reached the top of the barricade and she could see the broad, meandering curve of water, Caitlin relaxed, letting the fear and threat and strangeness of the evening recede. There was something about the river that always calmed her, settled her, made her feel at peace. Beside her, she felt the live tension in Ryder uncoiling, as well.

They walked without speaking to the railing and stopped, looking out over the water. The river lapped at the shore, and the city lights shimmered on the waves under the moon. The air was soft and warm and alive, moist like breath.

Caitlin could feel that Ryder was struggling with

something. Finally he spoke. "Why does he call you 'little sister'?"

That wasn't what she'd been expecting him to say at all. Caitlin shook her head. "He calls me all kinds of things. It doesn't mean anything. We're not related, if that's what you're asking."

"No, that I got," Ryder said ironically, and Caitlin blushed, realizing he'd figured out their relationship, or ex-relationship.

"I was young," she said defensively. "It's easy to get caught up when someone can shift and—" She stopped, mortified at what she'd just revealed.

He grinned at her. "And become anyone you want them to be?" he teased. And then he became serious. "You've got to watch the ones who don't know who they are at the core, that's all, Cait. And that's true of all men, not just shifters. You need to trust yourself to know what's right. You *can* trust yourself, you know."

Caitlin was unbelievably uncomfortable with the conversation, not knowing what to think. "I'm supposed to trust what a shifter says about shifters?"

"You should trust yourself," he said again, seriously. "Ask your heart."

That's all very well coming from someone who has no heart, she thought, but this time she didn't speak.

She didn't need him to be serious or compassionate or whatever he was being. She needed…

It was better not to think about what she was needing right now.

Suddenly she found herself being honest. "Case is a lost cause. Anyone can see that."

"And you're the patron saint of lost causes."

"I work with shifters, it's an occupational hazard."

He laughed, a deep, warm, real laugh. "Fair enough."

"But Danny…" She found herself dangerously close to tears and willed them away. "He's gifted," she finished shortly.

"Most shifters are." Something stole over Ryder's face, something so subtle it might just have been a shadow. But Caitlin felt a difference, something significant. His voice took on an edge. "But they can't hold the center. It's intoxicating to shift, the feel of weightlessness, the rush of being in the astral, being pure energy, completely light, more and less than human. And the power of manipulating human beings, of becoming whatever they desire, and seeing them helpless to resist you…"

His voice was far away. Caitlin felt a chill at his words, but she knew the chill was at least half excitement.

"It becomes an addiction, that power, the sensation,

all of it. And one addiction leads to another...." He trailed off, and his face hardened. "And a shifter who's opened himself too many times becomes open to all kinds of things. Including entities."

The agony in his voice was unmistakable, and Caitlin realized that he must be talking about someone he knew, someone close. She stared into the dark water beneath her, grappled with a dozen mental questions, finally asked carefully, "Is this really a job for you? Or was there something else?" She hesitated. "Some*one* else?"

He looked at her in the dark, seeming for a moment startled...and then not. "My sister," he said heavily. "I left home when I was just a teenager. She was much younger, and I rarely saw her. I could never stay in one place."

His mouth quirked bitterly. "I won't lie. I haven't been a saint. I had the same demons as any shifter, and I've used all my skills in every way they can be used. I've been a terror—for women, for humans in general."

Caitlin stared out at the reflected lights, silent, her thoughts racing. It was nothing she hadn't known about him—all the things that made him dangerous, that made her want to run from him. Still, she was shocked that he was being so open, so forthcoming. More than that, she could feel his pain, feel what was yet to come in the story.

"Little sister," she murmured.

"Yes, my little sister." There was such emotion on his face that his features seemed insubstantial, on the verge of shift. "While I was out raising hell all over the world, my little sister found *friends* like yours back there, and they got her started down a path that took over her life—and soul." His voice was bitter. "I didn't know, and if I had known, I'm not sure I would have cared. I had my own poisons."

He gripped the railing in front of them, and Caitlin was silent, letting him gather himself to continue again.

"I was lucky. A shifter who had been through the same journey that I had found me. He said I could do better with my gifts. He hired me and trained me for the work I do now—tracking, containing, casting out. And then one night I heard her…in the astral."

His face was so haunted that Caitlin had to keep herself from reaching out, touching him…. She grasped the railing and was silent.

"I heard my sister crying…and I knew it was her, and I knew I had to go to her." And now there were tears in his eyes, grief in his voice. "And then I heard the raging of that…thing." The loathing seethed through his entire body. Caitlin remembered how he had leaped out of his chair when that alien voice had come through Danny, the fury on his face, the killing rage….

"I was too late. She was young, by shapeshifter terms, and her body was weak from the drugs she'd been doing. That…*entity* got into her and burned through her like wildfire. She was dead before I could get there."

Caitlin felt a sharp stab of pain. She knew too well how it felt just to have a sister threatened. To lose one…to miss the chance of saving Fiona or Shauna… She shivered, her heart aching for him. "I'm so sorry," she murmured. Her hands stirred on the rail, wanting to reach for him, but she kept them still.

Ryder nodded but didn't look at her. He was a million miles away, staring out over the black and rippling water. So Caitlin kept her hands where they were and said nothing.

Chapter 15

It was a silent walk back to the compound, Ryder sunk in thought, and Caitlin not knowing what to say. It was a relief to reach the gate.

She stopped in front of it, drawing herself up. "Okay, you've walked me home. I'm fine. You can—"

"Come in and say good-night to your sisters," Ryder said unexpectedly, and reached past her to push the gate open.

Caitlin was reeling that the gate was unlocked, thinking that either her sisters had gone crazy to make a mistake like that, or that Ryder could actually open gates without that little tool of his...and then she realized the gate had actually opened from inside, and Shauna was standing there, looking royally pissed. "Of all the stupid, thoughtless, insensitive stunts…!"

Fiona was right behind her, nudging Shauna aside with a warning look. "All right, all's well that ends well."

Fiona shot Ryder a grateful look as she hugged and kissed Caitlin, and as soon as her sister's arms went around her, Caitlin felt a wave of guilt. She hadn't meant to cause anyone any grief, but then again, she never meant harm with anything she did, and somehow it always ended in disaster anyway.

"I'm sorry," Caitlin mumbled.

"Where *were* you?" Shauna demanded.

"We did find the shifters. And we did learn some fairly interesting things," Ryder said, stepping in smoothly, and Caitlin was aware that on some level he was trying to help her off the hot seat.

Well, fine, let him explain, then.

She shot Ryder a chilly look. "You can fill them in. I'm going to bed." And before anyone could say a word to stop her, she was stalking toward her wing of the house, fleeing through the garden toward welcome solitude.

In her bedroom, she jerked impatiently at the laces of her bodice, roiling with uncontrolled thoughts and feelings. As she pulled the dress over her head, she smelled the acrid residue of crack smoke clinging to the fabric and felt a stab of guilt, unease, even fear. For a moment she could hear the seething hatred of the thing that had spoken through Danny.

She tossed the dress aside with revulsion, wrapped her short silk robe around her and stepped to the French doors to look up at the moon, brooding.

There was a bigger malevolence to these entities than she had realized. The one they had talked to through Danny had a controlled, cunning plan to wreak havoc. And that very same entity had killed Ryder's sister. That fact gave the whole convergence of forces a fatedness that Caitlin was not about to take lightly.

She turned from the French doors—and almost screamed.

Ryder was standing in the middle of her bedroom floor, watching her.

She bit back the scream and crossed her arms, glaring at him. "Can you walk through walls now?"

"Spiders, remember?" he answered, arms crossed, looking down at her. "I don't usually do arachnids, but I needed something quick and small. And it's very easy to shift right now…."

Samhain, she thought.

"Oh. Right," she conceded sullenly. "Well, you can't just walk in anywhere you want to. It's trespassing."

She moved to step around him, but he sidestepped with her, blocking her.

"I'll leave if you want me to. The thing is…" He moved in closer, almost touching her. "I don't think you want me to."

She could feel the heat of his whole body resonating against hers. Another inch and he would be brushing against her, and her whole being seemed concentrated in that hot core of her.

"And *I* certainly don't want to," he added huskily.

She wasn't breathing now, and her entire skin seemed magnetically drawn to his, and yet he didn't touch her.

"Tell me not to kiss you," he said.

"Don't kiss me," she said, and closed her eyes as his mouth crushed down on hers.

His lips were hot and demanding; his hands were on the curve of her butt, pulling her against him, grinding sensuously through the thin cloth of her robe; and she was making those animal sounds again.

"God," he said roughly against her ear, and then she felt his tongue slide down her neck and she nearly fainted, except that his arm around her waist kept her upright.

Her breasts were straining under his hands, her nipples hard pellets of sensation. He ripped open her robe and closed his mouth around her left breast, sucking and licking until she was moaning…. She tried to push him away, but she had no strength in her arms. Her nails dug into his shoulder, and he transferred his mouth to the other breast, his hair brushing her skin as he tongued her aching nipple.

His hand slid between her legs, pulling her panties aside, and his thumb was stroking her then, his fingers dipping into her hot wetness, and she arched her back, moving in rhythm with his fingers, her breath coming short and fast as she felt her orgasm spiraling up through her, coiling her body as her muscles contracted in waves of heat and her wetness poured down his fingers. He groaned, lifting his head from her breast and covering her mouth with his, invading her with his tongue as he lowered her down onto the edge of the bed.

As she sank back in delirious exhaustion, he pulled her robe off her shoulders, tossing it against the wall, then stood to strip off his pants. He was huge; the thick length of him engorged, his pelvic muscles taut and cut, his abs jumping with the tension of his desire.

She pushed herself up on her elbows and edged back instinctively, overwhelmed by the hard maleness of him, the unmistakable purpose in his eyes.

He grabbed her ankles and pulled her down to the edge of the bed, took her wrists and held them above her head as he pushed her thighs apart with one knee, and now the head of his shaft was brushing against her sex, teasing her swollen flesh, stroking the cleft of her as she arched her back, straining toward him, incoherent, begging him, "Please…please…" And then he thrust forward and drove the length of him into her hot wetness, and she cried out with the rough friction against her sensitized flesh, the waves of sensation already building as he plunged into her. She was filled to overflowing, insane with the pleasure of his hugeness inside her, the weight of him on top of her, the stroke of his naked skin against hers. And then the wave broke and she was gasping in tandem with his growl of release, the hot waves of his pleasure as she contracted compulsively around him…both of them crying out in rhythm as their bodies spasmed together.

They sank into her pillows, sweating, panting, shaking…. Caitlin felt raw, more naked than she had ever been, completely stripped, exposed to her very core.

Ryder reached over and took her face in his hands as he wrapped a leg possessively around her, drawing her body against his as he kissed her mouth, her brow, her eyes.

"You are so lovely."

Chapter 16

She was half asleep, but she could tell that she was in bed, naked and wanton from a second bout of lovemaking. She felt raw and tender inside, but still hungry. Ryder was kissing her breasts, her neck, and crazily, she felt her nipples harden again, her sex start to ache. His fingers slipped between her legs, stroking and teasing until she moaned and opened under him…and then he was moving on top of her, pinning her with the weight of him. She was incoherent now, begging for him, and he shoved his hands under her, lifted her buttocks in both hands and thrust himself in to the hilt, filling her with his throbbing heat….

Her eyes were closed as she writhed against the pillows, gasping as each hot thrust took her to the edge of madness….

She opened her eyes…and saw a demonic face, monstrous, forked tongue waggling, vile with lust.

She screamed.

Someone was shaking her then, calling her name. "Cait. Cait!"

She scrambled up in terror, pressing her back against the headboard of the bed, eyes wide with shock.

"*Cait*," Ryder said. "It's not real. You were dreaming."

She gasped, let her breath out shakily, as she recognized her own room around her and saw Ryder kneeling on the bed beside her, freaked.

"Oh, God," she managed shakily. Gently he pulled her into his arms, and she slowly settled against his chest, felt his heart beating in time with hers, strong and real.

"I'm sorry," she said automatically, and he tensed.

"You have nothing to be sorry about." He pulled back slightly so he could look down at her. "You've been through way too much in the last few days. It's about time you got frightened."

She felt an uncomfortable wave of vulnerability

and tried to pull back from him, but he held her more firmly.

"Oh, no. You stay here. No pulling away." He leaned back and cuddled her against him until she breathed out and relaxed into him, letting him hold her. "Better," he whispered, kissing her hair.

She shivered violently. "It was that thing. It was trying to get inside me. Forcing itself inside me. It was horrible." To her chagrin, she found herself in tears. Ryder held her closer. "I knew it would kill, that it *wanted* to kill me."

She twisted in his arms and looked at him. "They don't care about staying in one body. They like burning through bodies. They'll never be satisfied. We have to stop them."

"We do," Ryder agreed. His face was troubled. "The question is, how? Mass exorcism? Mass binding? I've never seen such a huge collection of entities before. They can be bound one at a time, but a whole flock of them..." His face was shadowed in the candlelight. "I don't know how to start."

"We need a council meeting," Caitlin said. "All the communities. Some of the vampires have been around for centuries. Someone must know how to stop them."

Ryder was silent beside her.

"What?" she asked softly.

"I'm not used to working with anyone," he admitted. "Much less a whole community."

Caitlin thought of her parents, the dream they had of the communities working together, working for peace, and felt for the first time that she might understand it.

"It's our best hope," she said, and meant it. Ryder was silent, but she felt his arms tighten around her, and she was overwhelmed by the desire to stay there, always stay exactly as they were. Her heart hurt with it.

Ryder put his hand to her face suddenly and turned her head toward him, looking deep into her eyes. "Yes," he said, and she had no time to wonder what he meant before he kissed her, and then she forgot everything else as her body rose to his.

When Caitlin woke again to soft daylight, Ryder was wrapped around her. She lay still, feeling the huge weight of him, the silky softness of his skin, the power in the bulging muscles in his arms and thighs, the enticingly flat plane of his stomach against her back.

She was sore all over, most especially inside. And she was dismayed to find the throbbing she felt between her legs was not just soreness but desire. She wanted more, wanted him again, wanted him to hold her down and take her, again and again and again, until she was begging him to stop....

Begging. Oh, she had begged, all right, but not for him to stop. She had begged him for more…and more and more.

Her face flamed, remembering. She felt exposed, vulnerable, owned, used, helpless. That was the worst. She felt dependent, weaker than she'd ever felt in her life. She needed him, craved him, and he could go away any second. He was a shifter; there was no way to trust him.

One inch, one breath at a time, she eased herself out of his arms until she was standing. She hadn't woken him, but she felt cold, bereft, and longed to throw herself back into bed—back into *his* bed, because it didn't even feel like her own bed anymore—back into his arms….

No.

She forced herself to back up quietly and slipped into the bathroom, where she showered in water as hot as she could make it, scrubbing herself raw, trying in vain to remove his touch from her skin.

Ryder woke luxuriously in a bed redolent with Caitlin's perfume and the smell of sex. His erection was hot and hard and throbbing with wanting her, and he growled in his throat and reached for her…to find nothing, no one.

He sat up, blinking against a shaft of light from the windows. He could feel no sense of her in the room or anywhere else, and heard nothing, either, but a slow drip from the shower.

Caitlin sat in Fiona's kitchen, dressed as austerely as she could manage in a black turtleneck and gray jeans, her hands wrapped around her third mug of coffee. She was wired and nervous as a cat, and every time she moved she could feel Ryder on top of her, and feel her face burn and her chest flush with heat.

Luckily Shauna was chattering on, filling the silence, but Caitlin had seen Fiona glance at her appraisingly several times already. No way to hide anything from her—ever.

Caitlin reached for a croissant and smothered it with raspberry jam. Her hands were shaking so much she could barely hold the knife.

The front door opened, and she jumped about a mile. All three sisters went still, listening, then relaxed as they heard male voices and then Jagger stepped through the kitchen door, followed by Ryder.

The shifter was freshly scoured, in a leather jacket and tight jeans, and Caitlin could smell the combination of leather and pheromones from where she sat. She felt her pulse jump and blood throb between her legs.

"Look what I found on the street," Jagger announced to the sisters. Ryder glanced at Caitlin, and her heart was in her throat. Every detail of last night was in his eyes as he looked at her; they might have been naked in her bedroom right there, and she wouldn't have stopped him if he took her on the kitchen table.

She looked away from him and gulped coffee.

"Excellent," Fiona enthused. She pressed a mug of coffee into Ryder's hands. "Can I make you an omelet? We have croissants and juice and pastries on the table."

"Just this for now," Ryder said, lifting the mug, and glanced innocently at Cait.

Shauna was already up, demanding of Jagger, "The autopsy?"

Jagger looked to the three sisters. "Some of the signs are there. Massive adrenaline spike. Heart failure."

"But the chemicals are wrong," Shauna finished for him. Jagger nodded silently.

"So it *was* a walk-in. Possessing a were." Shane scowled.

"Which means even the Others are at risk," Fiona said tensely.

"Not just at risk," Ryder said. "If the lead entity has been hiding in one body, it may be using the body of an Other."

"It could be anyone, then," Shauna said.

"Hiding in plain sight," Ryder said, underlining the possibility.

"We need the Council to meet tonight," Caitlin said. "We can't wait."

"Yes," Jagger said.

The five of them looked around at each other, and Fiona suddenly stood up from the table. "Then let's do it."

Caitlin saw Ryder meet Jagger's eyes, glance toward the door. Neither of her sisters saw it, she realized.

Jagger stepped over to Fiona. "I have a full day—is there anything you need from me?"

"Go," Fiona said. "I'll call Armand, and we'll send out a summons. All you have to do is show up."

As Fiona started to walk Jagger to the door, Ryder looked toward Shauna and asked casually, "Bathroom?"

Shauna pointed. "First door to the left."

Caitlin pretended not to watch as Ryder walked casually out. She started clearing the table and then slipped out after him.

She hurried into the hall just in time to see Ryder shift.

She'd seen Case and Danny shift before, but as accustomed as she was to weirdness in her role as a Keeper, to other facets of reality, witnessing a shift was always unnerving. She wasn't sure if other, less attuned people would experience it in the same way, but for herself, she felt a queasy sense of not just the shifter but all of reality shifting around her, a momentary dissolving of anything concrete and tangible, while the shifter's body rearranged its molecules into something else entirely.

It happened now, and the nausea was instantaneous and racking as Ryder...melted, which was as close as her rational brain could come to describing it, and then there was a raven there in his place, a huge black bird, and he was flying out the open French doors and over the courtyard.

The room slowed its shimmering and returned to something resembling normal.

Caitlin held on to the wall and gagged from the dizziness, the overwhelming feeling of vertigo....

Then she forced herself to straighten and bolted toward the stairs after him.

Jagger waited on the outside of the compound wall, beside the gate. He turned at the rustle of wings as the raven landed on the gate, and then the air shimmered and Ryder stood in front of him.

The men regarded each other warily.

Jagger was the first to speak.

"I gather you don't think much of this plan."

Ryder shrugged. "Too many cooks."

Jagger's face tightened. "That's the way this city

works. The communities work together. That's how we keep the peace: coexistence."

"Yes, yes, very high-minded of you all, and I'm just a lone gunman. But the only thing I think this meeting is useful for is to see if a walk-in shows up in the body of one of your friends."

Slipping through the front door, Caitlin willed her feet to step lightly and ran at her most silent across the courtyard, coming to an abrupt halt just behind the wall, with the fountain providing cover so she could listen to the two men standing just outside the gate.

Ryder looked to the vampire and kept his voice level. "Do what you have to do, it's your city. But you have to know this. It's the Keepers who are the most vulnerable here."

He saw Jagger tense with suspicion as well as with worry, and felt a stab of satisfaction as he continued inexorably. "And not just Caitlin but all three of them. The lead entity is already aware of Caitlin, has directly threatened her twice, and I'd be shocked if it doesn't know of all of them. So do what you need to do, bring others into it, have your Council meeting, but know that every second we don't take action is giving these things an opening, and your woman is in the direct line of fire—just like mine."

* * *

Behind the fountain, Caitlin's heart leaped at his words. *His woman? Is it true? Is that how he thinks of me?* She eased closer to the wall to make sure she heard everything.

"Your woman?" Jagger was saying contemptuously. "Don't tell me you intend to stick around town after you've done what you came to do."

Ryder was silent, and Caitlin's heart plummeted. Finally he muttered, "What I do, where I stay, is none of your business, vampire."

"It *is* my business if it has to do with Cait," Jagger said coldly. "She's family now, my sister."

Caitlin felt a strange disorientation, a burning in her chest. *His sister? Me?*

Jagger continued. "You may have no conception of family, but make no mistake, shifter, I'll kill anyone who even thinks of hurting her."

Ryder was surprisingly and uncharacteristically silent. Behind the wall, Caitlin held her breath, hoping for him to jump in, to say something, anything….

Nothing but silence and the soft rustling of the wind in the trees.

Jagger snorted contemptuously. "As I suspected. So I'm telling you now. If your intentions aren't honorable, back off from Caitlin. Leave her free to find her own happiness. She deserves that."

Caitlin felt hot tears in her eyes, but what was

making her cry, she couldn't have said. Jagger's words…or Ryder's silence? She only knew she felt torn up inside.

And still nothing but silence from beyond the wall.

And then—finally—Ryder said, "I'll leave her alone, *brother*. Just don't interfere with my investigation."

Caitlin felt his words like a white-hot blow. *He doesn't care, then. It was nothing serious. He was only toying with me, and Jagger knew it.*

She felt as if her whole heart had dropped out of her body, felt like a complete fool, used and discarded like so much garbage.

"Right," Jagger said. "I'll see you tonight, then."

"I'll be there," Ryder answered roughly, and then Caitlin heard footsteps, two sets going in opposite directions, quickly fading down the street.

She leaned back against the fountain, sick with betrayal—and grief.

Somehow she made her way back to Fiona's rooms, knowing that she had to go on, to act as if everything was normal and fine. She had to make everyone think she was all right.

The table was already cleared, the dishes put away, and Fiona and Shauna were in the living room, talking, Shauna as usual prowling the room like a wild animal. She stopped in her tracks when Caitlin entered from the garden door.

"And where did you just go off to? Or should I say '*get* off'? What's going on with you and that shapeshifter, anyway?"

Her younger sister wasn't teasing. Caitlin could feel the sharpness of the question underneath the joke.

"Nothing's going on with him," Caitlin said coldly. "He has prior knowledge of the walk-ins. We need to know what he knows, whatever he's telling the truth about, which may not be much. That's all."

Sensing a storm brewing, Fiona stepped in smoothly. "We need a Council meeting. I for one think Mallory is telling the truth, and we need to prepare ourselves, and root out these walk-ins any way we can." She looked at Caitlin penetratingly as she asked the next question.

"You don't have any reason to doubt that whatever happens will happen on Samhain, do you?"

Caitlin met her eyes, answered reluctantly. "No. I think we need to be ready for a mass possession on Samhain, if we don't act before then."

Fiona looked at both her sisters. "Then let's move."

Chapter 17

Ever since restaurateur Armand St. Pierre had assumed the position of head counselor of the shapeshifting community, shifter-called Council meetings had taken on a sumptuous elegance far beyond the usual freewheeling style of the Communities. St. Pierre owned the historic restaurant Viola's, catercornered to Jackson Square. It had been an old Creole mansion, and now the downstairs rooms served as an upscale restaurant—closed to the public tonight—famous for its Sunday jazz breakfasts, and the upper level, with its polished cypress floors and enormous fireplaces in every room, was rented out as a banquet hall for parties. It was a perfect gathering place for Council meetings, as the upstairs had several discreet back entrances, and the entire floor was completely private, its own self-contained universe, more than big enough for the dozens of Others who gathered for a meeting of the appointed Council representatives of the various races. And the food St. Pierre provided was so excellent that not even the werewolves complained about the upper-crust surroundings.

Caitlin loved Viola's because of its timelessness. The upstairs was like a tour through history: the stairwell where Gregorian chants played continuously, so softly, subconsciously, that it felt like a dream, like ghost music; the red-wallpapered Victorian bordello rooms with their gilt mirrors and horsehair couches, and even an Egyptian sarcophagus; and the elegant banquet halls, one room flowing into another with twenty-foot-tall doors separating them, and marble fireplaces in each hall.

When St. Pierre hosted, he demanded formal dress at the Council meetings. While there was no way technically to enforce the dress code, New Orleans residents being costume fetishists at heart, a surprising number of the Others complied, even went full-out and got competitive in their period elegance.

Armand particularly expected to see the three Keepers setting the bar in the costume department, and even Shauna, who favored jeans and tank tops, would not have denied him. If a little lace and perfume kept the shapeshifters' high counsel happy, it was worth an extra hour spent dressing.

And despite the seriousness of the occasion, after phoning, emailing and racing around the city all day to ensure that all the Council members would be present at the impromptu summit, all three Keepers were looking forward to a party.

The MacDonald sisters, particularly Fiona, had a long-term association with the best costumer in the Quarter, Rosalyn Connor, who met the three sisters at Viola's with some of her best vintage Creole finery.

Now Caitlin stood in one of the bordello rooms with her hands propped against the wall as Fiona laced her up into a corset. Rosalyn was handling Shauna, who muttered darkly about this part, but Caitlin loved the pretty clothes and the excuse to wear them. Rosalyn had as usual outdone herself, and the sisters' dresses were beaded confections of silver, lilac and gold.

"Someone could try explaining to me how these instruments of torture are supposed to help us think better," Shauna grumbled, as Rosalyn yanked her corset strings. "Cutting off the oxygen to our brains…"

"Anything that will make you talk less and listen more," Fiona said tartly.

"Hah-hah." Shauna pulled away from Rosalyn and adjusted her bosom, unperturbed. She glanced in the mirror, and Caitlin could see she wasn't displeased with what she saw; the golds and reds of her gown made her exotic coloring shimmer.

"Thanks, Roz. You're a miracle." Shauna kissed the costumer's cheek quickly, and escaped the room.

Fiona had finally finished Caitlin's stays and tied them off, tucking the strings into the bodice. "That was too easy," she said to Caitlin, frowning. "You're not eating, are you?"

Rosalyn was pulling the silver dress off the form that had held it. "Girls in love don't eat," the irrepressible costumer quipped, and Caitlin felt herself redden. Luckily Rosalyn had already dropped the dress over her head, so no one could see the tears springing to her eyes.

He doesn't want me. It's just a job. She swallowed and forced a scoffing tone. "With a shapeshifter? Not in this lifetime," she retorted, her voice muffled under yards of gossamer fabric.

Beyond the dress, there was a suspicious silence. Caitlin felt hands tugging the gown down over her corset and petticoats, and as her head and shoulders emerged, she caught a glimpse of Fiona giving Rosalyn a significant look.

Rosalyn snatched up a velvet shawl and said

loudly, "That Shauna—she left behind the most important part. You can button the dress for Cait, can't you?" she said to Fiona, and promptly headed for the door, tossing a "You look beautiful, baby," over her shoulder as she bustled out.

Caitlin's eyes narrowed. "I know you two are up to—" Then Fiona turned Caitlin toward the mirror, and Caitlin fell silent as she saw herself in shimmering silver. It was a stunning dress; she felt as beautiful as she'd ever felt in her whole life.

"It would be a shame to waste all that gorgeousness tonight," Fiona remarked, as she started to do up the buttons.

"Are you pushing me toward a shifter?" Caitlin demanded in disbelief. "I swear, that vampire has fried your brain."

"I'm not pushing anyone anywhere," Fiona demurred.

Liar. But I'm just not like you. No one will ever feel that way about me.

"And don't call him 'that vampire,'" her sister added, with a coolness that made Caitlin pause. Fiona so rarely lost her temper that Caitlin knew to be very careful if there was even a hint that she might.

"Sorry," Caitlin muttered, and turned away, tucking her gris-gris bag into the bodice of her dress.

Fiona sighed. "Caitlin, we work with Others. We will always work with Others. But even if we didn't, are we really serving anyone by thinking of them as Others to begin with? We share the planet with them. We share this city with them. We want the same things—music, good food, good times. Happiness. *Love*." She paused.

"I know you've been hurt," she continued carefully, and her hands were gentle as she continued to button the dress up Caitlin's back. "But you could have been hurt just as hard by a mortal. We fall in love, we make mistakes—that's life. We're all doing the best we can."

Caitlin found her throat aching, tears pushing at her eyes.

Fiona laughed softly. "It's scary, isn't it?"

Caitlin nodded, unable to speak.

"Every day since I met Jagger, I'm scared to death," Fiona said, but she was laughing as she spoke, her happiness evident.

Choked up though she was, Caitlin was able to laugh with her.

Fiona hugged her from behind.

"This shifter—you may not think so, but he cares about you. He *sees* you." She paused, glanced in the mirror at their dual reflection, and continued wryly. "And you're not always the easiest person to get." She stopped again, then continued slowly. "But I think he does. And sometimes love is about someone who is willing to see you—and love you despite everything."

Caitlin's emotions were roiling, and she didn't trust herself to speak. Fiona was almost never wrong. Could she possibly be right, now?

Fiona had reached the top button, and now she smoothed down the back of Caitlin's gown with a satisfied look in the mirror.

"All I want is for you to be happy. And you'll never be happy without someone who's your equal—and who loves you. That's all I'm saying, and I'll stop now. It's all about love."

The sisters were silent, looking at each other in the mirror, through a shimmer of candlelight—and tears.

Ryder milled in the throngs of Others crowding the elegant rooms of Viola's, experiencing a heady rush of memories, all the reasons he had always loved New Orleans.

For someone who had lived almost two centuries, the city was an intoxicating mix of the old and the new. Ryder's nostalgia and his hunger for new ideas were equally satisfied and stimulated by the mix of styles, foods, music and attendees at this sumptuous party. Armand St. Pierre was a superlative host. No surprise. Beings who had lived through several generations became adept at culling the most intriguing, lavish, stimulating, daring trends of each era and combining them to create multilayered extravaganzas of visual, sensual, auditory, olfactory and gastronomic sensations.

Without ever forgetting his purpose there, which was to suss out any signs of possession by a walk-in, Ryder delighted in the pleasures around him: the costuming, the impeccably trained waitstaff, the perfect restoration of a building that had been just as lovely nearly a century ago, when it had been the private residence of an old New Orleans family and Ryder had attended a Christmas ball there. By New Year's he had been run out of town by the male relatives of the young debutante he had met at that party...

But that had been another era.

Earlier he had seen Shauna dash by in a rush of scarlet and gold, but there had been no sign of the other Keepers. Focused as he was on the task of recognizing any signs of walk-in possession among the other guests, he felt equally tense about seeing Caitlin again.

As he thought it, his eye was drawn up the sweeping staircase—and his heart almost stopped at the sight.

Caitlin was standing at the top of the stairs, poised and still, looking down over the crowd as if taking it in, taking a breath, before her descent.

She was unbelievably beautiful in a gown sparkling with crystals that made her look like starlight. Almost two hundred years, and Ryder couldn't remember seeing anyone, anything, like her.

She took a breath that he felt in his own chest and started down the stairs, not at a walk, but floating, a queen descending to her destiny.

He stepped forward to claim her.

Standing on the stairs, Caitlin felt the warmth of the room flowing up toward her, a wave of mingled sensual delights.

Everything below her was candlelight and lamplight. Armand had the most demanding taste and would never allow anything less than period perfection at his parties.

The smells of seafood and sausage, delicate she-crab soup and set-your-mouth-on-fire gumbo, fresh fruit, burnt sugar, chocolate, fragrant flowers and sensual perfumes drifted in the air, which shimmered with candlelight and anticipation. And for a moment Caitlin understood that the Others *kept* the mysterious history of New Orleans, just as the Keepers kept the balance between the needs of the Others and humankind.

And then she felt a rush of heat beyond the pleasing glow of fires in the massive fireplaces, beyond the wavering of candles and the sparkle of champagne and good food and good music and good times.

She focused below her and saw…Ryder Mallory

standing at the bottom of the stairs and looking straight up at her.

He was dressed in an embroidered waistcoat, probably something Armand had forced on him; St. Pierre was notorious for pulling his guests aside at the door and providing a costume to suit his ideas of proper dress. Caitlin knew he kept a superbly stocked dressing room for just that purpose.

But Ryder wore the finery as if he had been born to it. The man who looked up at her—waiting for her—was no rogue, but royalty. And the intention on his face, in his eyes, was breathtaking. His desire was as clear as if he were speaking aloud, not simple desire for her body, but for her entire being. Caitlin slowed on the stairs, overwhelmed by the power of it—and at the same time acutely aware of her own power over him.

She stopped on the bottom step, and Ryder moved forward and bowed as if he had done it every day of his life—then held out an arm to lead her down the last stair. Caitlin rested her hand lightly on his arm, feeling that electric jolt between them.

His eyes were fixed on hers as if he would never look away. "You are the loveliest thing in this room," he said, without a trace of irony, and Caitlin felt herself blush from the top of her breasts to her cheeks, a high, erotic flame. "And the loveliest woman I have ever seen," he added softly, and she felt her insides dissolve, her head spin.

She had no idea how to respond to him, or even how she was going to remain standing in the intense focus of his wanting. It was a moment stopped in time; there were other bodies, other beings, around them, but they were alone in the room, alone in the universe.

"We have work to do," she said.

Although she could see from his face that he understood completely that she was deliberately breaking the moment, unable to handle its implications, he remained gravely courteous. There was not a trace of mockery in his voice when he answered, "Yes. I've been walking the room. So far nothing suspicious, no one out of control or acting any more strangely than Others tend to act at a party."

"That's good," she answered, aware of how awkward the nuts-and-bolts conversation was, considering their circumstances and attire. She felt as if she were trapped in a movie, playing a role that was layered over the truth of what she wanted to live.

"How do these Council meetings work?" he asked, looking at her mouth as he spoke. She tried to focus… but all she wanted was for him to kiss her.

"We'll be called to dinner, and then the meeting will start over dessert," she answered him, forcing herself to stay calm.

"We have time, then," he said, and her chest flushed and her heart began to race.

Time for what?

She had a sudden vision of him sweeping her up, carrying her up the stairs like Scarlett O'Hara, throwing her down on one of the Victorian couches, tearing open her gown and ravishing her over and over and over again....

He smiled slowly, as if he'd seen—and lived— every moment of her brief fantasy along with her. Then he said with maddening casualness, "Time to mingle and check out the guests, I meant."

"Of course," she said, her face burning.

"Tell me who I should know here," he suggested. "One of your Community leaders would be an ideal host to possess, if the walk-in we're after could manage it."

Caitlin forced herself to focus on the room, the other guests. "You met our host at the door, I'm sure," she said, nodding toward Armand St. Pierre. The shapeshifter was resplendent in a purple frock coat, high boots and breeches.

"Yes, and in a previous life, as well," Ryder told her. Caitlin looked at him curiously. Ryder was sure she knew part of the story. St. Pierre had been openly homosexual in a time when that orientation could bring on persecution, beatings, loss of property, arrest, even murder. He had been a leader of the homosexual elite in New Orleans at the turn of the century and provoked dissent among the shapeshifters of the time, when they felt his open lifestyle might also call attention to the shapeshifter presence in the community.

St. Pierre was unbowed by pressure from any side, however, and the gay community in New Orleans owed him more of a debt than any mortal probably realized.

But Ryder knew something about the elegant shifter that few did—Others or human. St. Pierre was an ailuranthrope, a cat shifter, and in younger days had used his talents in the sex trade to satisfy the most exotic and outré tastes. It was said that there was no desire too outrageous to be fulfilled in the French Quarter, and shapeshifters had helped build that reputation. Armand and the stable he gathered had catered to the most…imaginative of clients. Armand himself was rumored to have been the most highly prized of all sex shifters.

Ryder stooped to whisper in Caitlin's ear, enjoying the heady fragrance of her perfume. As he spoke, he felt her breath stop. Her eyes widened and met his. "I swear it's true," he said.

"Cat sex," Caitlin marveled.

"Don't knock it till you've tried it," he said, looking down at her, and enjoying the color that flushed across her décolletage.

She turned quickly away from his gaze, looking out over the crowd, trying to reroute the conversation.

"That big were over there is Danyon Stone, alpha of the West Bank were-pack."

Ryder recognized the young man instantly—the one who had nearly killed him in the abandoned house earlier that day.

"Yes, that one I'm familiar with, as well," he said dryly.

Even if he hadn't seen the were midchange, he could have identified his species instantly; there was something about a were that stood out, and not just to shapeshifters. Many a time Ryder had observed mortals unconsciously steering clear of werewolves as they passed them on the street, especially on days or nights close to the full moon. Humans hadn't entirely lost their own animal instincts.

"There are six wolf packs in the parish, each with its own alpha," Caitlin continued. She searched the room until she found a commanding young woman. She nodded to Ryder, and waited until his eyes followed hers and stopped on the young woman. "That's Kara Matiste, East Bank alpha."

"Weres have come up in the world," Ryder said. When last he'd been in New Orleans, werewolves weren't anything near organized; they ran like, well, wolves, and took suggestions from no one. These two alphas stood out from the crowd; while they were dressed in period clothes, there was still something rough about them—wolves in sheep's clothing.

"The alphas control the packs, but everyone answers to August, as you know from this afternoon." Again she searched the crowd, until she found the dignified, craggy-faced man, now deep in conversation with Shauna. Caitlin briefly touched Ryder's arm. The touch made Ryder look not at Gaudin but at her, a penetrating look that left no doubt as to where his true focus was that evening. Caitlin blushed and inclined her head toward the were, and finally Ryder looked. Even this distinguished lawyer had a wolfish face, Ryder thought. *Classic were.* He wasn't surprised to hear that Gaudin was the acting head of the were-council and responsible for and to all the were-packs of the community. Any werewolf who had managed to stay alive as long as Gaudin had possessed superior skills; wolves' lives tended to be nasty, brutish and short.

The vampires were also easily distinguishable. Ryder had found there was a marble quality to their features, a chiseled look and fashionable gauntness that made them electrifying standouts in any crowd.

"Jagger you know," Caitlin said, nodding; the vampire detective was of course glued to Fiona's side, and Ryder didn't blame him. The eldest Keeper was stunning in a lilac gown; no woman in the room could rival her—except the one at Ryder's own side.

"And that's David Du Lac. He owns a jazz club—on Frenchmen Street, though, not Bourbon—and David's the real deal. He and Jagger are friends. They've been through fire together. David is acting head of the vampires."

"Who's the twitchy one?" Ryder asked, and didn't even have to point out the one he meant, the one he'd noticed from the moment he'd walked into the room.

Caitlin knew exactly who he was asking about; she wrinkled her nose in a way Ryder would have found endearing if she weren't so obviously distressed.

"Banjo Marks," she said with distaste.

"Bad news," Ryder said.

"Oh, yeah," she answered fervently.

"Surprised he even has a seat, here." It *was* surprising. Jagger DeFarge was a model citizen—more than a model citizen, a pillar of the community, dedicated to serving the humans of the city as well as his own kind. After seeing the vampire in action, Ryder had expected the other Council members to be, if not equally exemplary, at least stable, as Du Lac certainly seemed to be.

But Marks... There was something about the skinny, nervous vampire that would have drawn Ryder's attention as trouble in any situation, and even more so in a gathering where he was on active lookout for a possessed Other.

Caitlin shook her head. "Banjo's from an old bayou family. You know how it is here—bloodlines are everything, even if you're a vampire."

But despite Marks's flamboyantly odd behavior, Ryder realized he was not the likeliest suspect in the room.

"So he's always like this?" he asked, and Caitlin began to answer.

"Worse than this, actually." And she stopped, and he saw she'd realized his point.

Quick study, this woman. A Keeper, he thought, to himself, but his feelings were too deep for the pun to be a joke.

"Yes," she said more slowly. "He's acting completely normal—for him."

"Right," Ryder said. "So probably not possessed. What we want is to keep looking for behavior that's beyond the norm for someone in particular."

He scanned the room again, noticing the shapeshifters in the crowd. The shapeshifters—now there was a different kind of charisma, less easily explained. When you looked at a shapeshifter, you saw what you wanted to see. Expert shifters—and there were no others at this gathering—could unconsciously pick up the fantasies of even random strangers and reflect a tantalizing fantasy persona right back at the wishful thinker. He'd done it often enough himself.

He suppressed a twinge of guilt and focused again on the crowd.

Notably absent were Caitlin's musician friends, Case and Danny. Too rebellious to do anything as mainstream as serve on the Council, obviously.

"Where are your friends?" he asked Caitlin anyway, straight-faced, and he saw her flare up, defensively.

"This isn't their kind of—" She stopped, realizing he was joking. "Very funny." Then she sighed. "Shapeshifters are so hard to recruit. Most of the Others have this natural wariness about the Council. It took a lot of years to get…most Others comfortable enough with our intentions to make any kind of parish-wide delegation at all. But shapeshifters…"

She stopped then, suddenly not wanting to say something insulting.

Instead of getting angry, he grinned at her. "Sorry bastards, all of us. Temperamental, self-righteous…" He dropped the joking tone and said more seriously, "It's what I said last night. When you've been so many people, your own sense of self gets hazy. It's hard for a shifter to trust anything. Anyone."

But the way he looked at her was not the look of someone who was distrustful.

"I'm sorry you ended up with the hardest-headed

group of Others out there," he said, and sounded so sincere that it nearly took her breath away. "On the other hand, I'm not sorry at all that it was you."

And the way he looked at her when he said that *did* take her breath away....

But the moment was broken and the bright, wine-enhanced party chatter suspended as an old-fashioned waiter—in a wig and doublets, snug-fitting Renaissance jacket, no less—rang an enormous dinner bell and announced, "Dinner is served."

Other wigged and doubleted servants pulled open the twenty-foot-tall doors, and the party began to flow into the dining hall, from which a current of savory smells rolled: gumbo and duck and raspberry and chocolate and butter and heavenly bread and the woodsy scent of a fire.

Ryder offered his arm to Caitlin with a slight bow. She felt the skin of her chest and shoulders flush—and not just from embarrassment. Underneath there was a sense of pride. Pride of ownership, and of being owned.

Which isn't true at all, she admonished herself. *It has nothing to do with anything.*

But that was the way Ryder was looking at *her*, too.

She put her hand on his well-muscled arm, and he swept her into the dining hall.

* * *

St. Pierre's love of ceremony extended to the seating; the tables were carefully laid out in a large rectangle, with Council delegates from each of the Other communities forming three sides of the rectangle, in descending order. The General Council members were seated at the head table, with St. Pierre in the middle, and the three Keepers to his right. Ryder, being the guest speaker as well as the guest of the Keepers, had a place between Caitlin and Fiona, a privilege that even Jagger couldn't claim; he sat with the vampires at the vampire table, and while he was playing it off with vampire cool, Ryder could feel he was steaming. Ryder wouldn't have been a shifter worth his salt if he didn't torture the vampire a little, leaning in to be extra attentive to the charming Fiona.

Who liked him, he could tell. And since Fiona was obviously Caitlin's father, mother, fairy godmother and sister all rolled into one, it was useful as well as a pleasure to be on her good side.

He liked Shauna, too—the youngest Keeper was a firecracker in an earthier way than the more ephemeral Caitlin. The sisters each bore at least some imprint of the Other community they represented. Occupational hazard, clearly.

The food was superb, but the formality of the dinner bothered Ryder. He continually had to restrain himself from feeding Caitlin oysters with his fingers, from kissing raspberry sauce from the corners of her mouth. He could imagine this sumptuous feast in private, where he could have his fill of her body along with the food. And he could feel her sense his thoughts, if not outright read them; he felt her attraction for him in the heat between them, in the chemicals of her body, creating an intoxicating pull, literally vibrating. Her body responded to even the slightest shifts in his posture, to the brush of his hand against her arm, to the graze of his thigh against hers under the table. He was having a great deal of fun tormenting her with his "accidental" touches…but truth be told, he was tormenting himself every bit as much. He was swollen with arousal beneath the tight breeches he wore, filled with a raw impatience to seize her, take her, standing, sitting, in his lap, splayed on the table under his thrusts…the taste of raspberry on her mouth…licking cream off her breasts…feeling the warm wetness of her engulfing him, driving him to the brink….

She had gone very still by his side, and when he looked at her, he had no doubt she knew exactly what he was thinking. He held her eyes without smiling, to emphasize the moment, the meaning that was passing between them.

She shoved her chair back abruptly, breaking the moment, and stood—shakily, he noted with satisfaction. She hurried from the table, and for now, he let her go. There was work to do; she would be in the spotlight soon in her official capacity. He understood that he had unbalanced her profoundly, and that she needed to regain her composure to do her work. Important work.

He noticed Fiona watching her go. Then she turned her eyes on him, and the look she gave him was appraising—and carried a cool and direct reminder of her words in the kitchen. *If you hurt her, you'll answer to me.*

Ryder met Fiona's eyes calmly and didn't look away. She nodded thoughtfully and turned back to her meal.

Ryder leaned back in his chair, marveling at how civilized the gathering seemed, how ordered. They were seated in a room full of supernatural entities that could easily run rampant through the human population of this city or any other, taking whatever vicious pleasure they wanted from whoever or whatever crossed their tracks. But what he saw was a citizenry that may have had its differences, but now was making efforts on many fronts to get along, to forge a general community, an alliance, despite something far stronger than racial or cultural differences: differences of species, of beingness.

He had come to understand that the sisters' parents had had much to do with the forging of this community spirit, and at great cost. But it was dawning on him now that the three sisters, these three young Keepers, might have done even more than their parents, and at a far younger age, to ensure the civilized functioning of the underworld.

Surprisingly, he felt drawn toward the idea, the warmth, of a community where everyone worked together for the common good. Where he might stop and stay, make a home and a life, instead of this incessant and angry wandering.

More surprising still, he was curious, even hungry, to know what it would be like to share a life's work with a lover and partner the way Caitlin's parents so clearly had, willing to risk their very lives for love of community, for a higher purpose, for love itself.

His thoughts were interrupted by the sudden sound of silver ringing on crystal. Armand St. Pierre had started the ancient summons to order by tapping a knife against a goblet, a perfect icy clarion call that silenced dinner chatter as effectively as a shot from a gun.

Armand acknowledged the effect with a small smile and stood theatrically, raising his glass.

"Brother and Sister Others. I welcome you to my table—and to the Council. The Keepers of the City of New Orleans and vampire liaison Jagger DeFarge have requested a special joint session of Council to discuss an imminent attack on our city."

Ryder frowned, looking toward the doors for Cait. Very strange, that St. Pierre would have started the meeting without her.

At his seat, St. Pierre continued. "I pray you listen with your hearts and minds, that we may keep the peace between us and the peace of the city."

St. Pierre took a long moment to look around the room before speaking again. "I give you Jagger DeFarge."

The vampire rose from his table and walked up to the podium that had materialized just to the left of the head table.

"My Brother and Sister Others," Jagger began formally, the same address that St. Pierre had used. "We are facing a great danger to our city. I hope that, as in previous times of attack, of threats to our balance, our way of life, we will put our differences aside and band together to repel this enemy."

Ryder had to admit that DeFarge cut a striking figure—and managed a stirring speech.

Perhaps there's something to this Council, after all, he mused. *A community of Others. Who'd have thought?*

Outside the banquet hall, Caitlin found refuge in the bathroom—a sumptuous affair that continued the Victorian theme. There were roses everywhere, in the wallpaper, carved into the light fixtures, tastefully arranged in crystal vases on the sinks and makeup table, in the paintings on the walls. The whole powder room radiated the fragrance of rose oil. It combined with her already overstimulated state to create...an even more overstimulated state.

Get a grip, she chided herself, staring into the golden rose-rimmed mirror. The modern words clashed absurdly with the period elegance of her dress and hair.

You have work to do. You can't go off the deep end about a man who will be gone with the wind—literally—tomorrow.

When she had pulled herself together enough to think about venturing back to the meeting, she breathed in and pulled the bathroom door open.

In the dark hall in front of her, a pale face moved abruptly forward, and she gasped, drawing back....

Armand St. Pierre stepped forward from the shadows.

"My dear, I'm so sorry to have frightened you,"

Caitlin relaxed, recognizing the shapeshifter. Then she immediately thought she must have missed something crucial, if the Council Chair was coming to get her. She began to apologize.

"I'm so sorry, I was just headed back—"

The elegant shapeshifter lifted a hand. "Not at all. The..." He paused, and there was something both delicate and loaded in the way he spoke the next words. "The *bounty hunter* will soon be speaking, and I was hoping to have the opportunity to talk with you alone first."

"Of course," she answered automatically, but with a sinking feeling. *Does he know Ryder? Is something wrong? Is everything about to crumble?*

"I am most appreciative," St. Pierre said graciously, and extended an arm, touching her back to lead her down the hall away from the dining room.

He unlocked a carved walnut door at the end of the corridor and ushered Caitlin into what could only have been his personal business office. There was a combination of elegance and authority about it—fine furnishings and antique office paraphernalia that belonged in a museum, but which were clearly not for show, seeing daily use in the running of the restaurant and business.

As soon as he closed the door behind them, Caitlin turned to him, too anxious to hold back the question.

"Do you know Ryder, then?"

St. Pierre laughed softly and extended a gracious hand toward the sitting area. "My dear, you and your sisters never cease to amaze me. The city has been in the most competent and lovely of hands ever since your ascension."

Caitlin had always been uncomfortable with the formality of St. Pierre's language, but she knew it was not an affectation; the shapeshifter was several centuries old.

Then something suddenly changed in his manner, and the flowery words were gone, as if he'd read her mind. "We won't mince words, however. You are correct. I do know the bounty hunter—from long ago—and I have grave doubts as to the veracity of the story he's bringing us."

Caitlin's heart sank…but in a way she had known, had always known. *Ryder. I knew I couldn't trust him. It's all been a lie.*

St. Pierre's eyes were keen on her face, absorbing her reaction. She knew he was reading what she was feeling.

"My dear, the last thing I would ever want is to see you or one of your sisters hurt. We had enough of a scare—just months ago, wasn't it? A near-lethal threat to both your sister and you?" He shook his head. "And I was every bit as shocked as you were that one of our own was the cemetery killer. I'm afraid that the more devious of my—our—kind can do untold damage. And I'm even more afraid that's precisely the case here."

Caitlin felt the pressure of growing horror and dismay. It was all her fault. She had so wanted to believe in Ryder…and in her fog of distraction, she had brought an insidious evil into the community.

"What…what do you know?" she asked, shakily.

"I know we must be rid of the bounty hunter to-night."

Her heart cried out that it could not be true. *Trust your heart,* Ryder's voice whispered to her. And in that moment Caitlin quieted her screaming thoughts, her roiling doubts, and listened, really listened, to the shapeshifter leaning toward her earnestly.

"He is a threat not only to our communities but, I am afraid, especially to you, and to your sisters...."

He spoke with utmost sincerity. But through his words Caitlin caught a sibilance that was familiar—and deadly. She kept her face still, with a fixed look of concern, as she looked behind St. Pierre, letting her eyes go unfocused so she could read the auric circumference around him.

And she caught a glimpse of a darkness so malevolent she had to keep herself from gasping out loud.

Commanding every muscle, every nerve, to be still, she said softly, "I've thought so all along. What can we do?"

"He'll have to die," St. Pierre said nonchalantly. "And now so will you, my dear."

His tone never changed, and it took a fraction of a second for Caitlin to register what he had just said.

Before her eyes, St. Pierre shifted from elegant host to something inconceivable...with fur, fangs, the malevolent eyes of a cat/predator...but there was something not at all catlike there, as well. There was no grace or symmetry; the creature that morphed before her was alien, ragged, demonic, repellent, a bestial horror. The body of a serpent and the paws of a cat, the talons of a falcon, the glittering eyes of a snake and the jaws of a lion…

And the voice that emanated from its mouth was grating, and horrifically familiar—the voice of the walk-in that had spoken through Danny the night before.

"Die, Keeper…"

The thing coiled itself like some lethal cobra, settling on taloned haunches…and sprang….

Chapter 18

In the banquet hall, vampire Mateas Grenard had the floor, and was speaking skeptically and somewhat pompously. "So far these 'walk-ins' have only possessed tourists, though, have they not? Humans? So what affair is it of ours? We don't interfere with human concerns."

Jagger kept his voice gracious—Ryder noted Jagger's Council manners were a bearing totally unlike his cop persona. "The fact that the entities are killing tourists is a threat to our Communities because tourist deaths in New Orleans mean big media attention. Do the Communities want to risk having the national media camping out in the Quarter?"

"And it's not just humans who have been killed. A were died yesterday morning, with the same symptoms as the human victims," the alpha were Danyon Stone said.

Grenard turned to Jagger with raised eyebrows. "You didn't mention that."

"That death is still under investigation."

Ryder watched from the head table as the werewolves' tempers flared. Already there were signs of imminent transmutation; he could see it in the features of the weres in front of him, thickening, coarsening, darkening with fur under the surface of the skin, fingernails sharpening.

This is going to get ugly, he realized. But it wasn't his Council, nor was it necessarily his problem. In fact, the heightened emotions playing out in front of him might reveal something useful, might draw something out. He could feel Fiona tensing beside him, and Shauna was already on her feet, moving toward the fray.

Ryder heard someone mutter, "A shapeshifter did it," and now he tensed. Not because he was afraid for himself, but because he knew full well how quickly different species of Others could turn on each other, and they had no time for infighting.

"Yes, what about the shapeshifter?" the female alpha were, Kara Matiste, growled. "That one—" she turned and pointed to Ryder "—shows up, and a were ends up dead, not to mention humans are dropping left and right. The timing is too obvious to be coincidental."

Ryder rose to speak, but Jagger shot him a warning look and held up his hands to calm the crowd. "Mallory is a bounty hunter, following the horde of entities. He arrived after the first tourist deaths."

"How do you know that?" Kara demanded. "How do you know he wasn't here and just in hiding? Can he prove it?"

"And why should we trust a vampire, anyway?" someone else muttered, but loudly enough to be heard.

The twitchy bayou boy, Marks, hissed disapproval at the insult, and now the vampires were standing, rallying.

Ryder suddenly felt a surge of adrenaline totally unrelated to the fight going on before him, a rush of sympathetic...terror was the only word. And not his own.

Caitlin's.

He stood, knocking back his chair, and surveyed the crowd in the banquet hall. No sign of her, and she had been gone a long time. Too long. He took in a quick panorama of startled faces, concerned ones, angry ones, accompanied by a rise of muttered questions and epithets at his sudden disruption of the already disrupted proceedings. Fiona, Shauna and Jagger had all turned to him with questioning eyes….

He ignored everyone and broke into a run toward the doors.

Inside Armand's office, Caitlin's frozen muscles unlocked and she bolted—not backward, but darting straight past the creature, the only way she could get to the door.

Already in midspring, the beast before her was too clumsy to recalibrate and landed heavily on gargoyle paws, colliding with the couch. Caitlin heard crashing, splintering, a roar of rage, as she scrabbled for the doorknob—and had a heart-stopping moment of finding it locked.

She could feel, rather than see, the creature behind her whipping its body around, serpentlike. And in a flash she remembered Ryder's charmed skeleton key, the one she'd been keeping in her gris-gris bag since he gave it to her that night off Bourbon Street.

She pulled the charm bag from her bodice and touched it to the knob, which clicked open instantly in her hand.

Caitlin ducked out of the door, feeling the claws of the creature ripping at her back as she fled.

In the dark corridor, she ran at full tilt toward the banquet hall, her breath coming in shaky gasps, her mind racing a mile a minute. *I can't lead it into the banquet hall. It could kill everyone.* She had felt the power emanating from the beast, not just the considerable power of the elder shapeshifter, but the raw demonic energy of the walk-in. It was a terrifying combination.

But those thoughts were eradicated by her primal need. *Ryder. I need Ryder.*

In the banquet hall, Shauna had gotten some control over the werewolves. She stood in the center of a shifting circle of weres, all of them much taller than she was at the moment, as their heightened emotions set off the transmutation.

"This killer is not someone from any of our communities," she reassured the weres loudly. "That's why we're here tonight."

Caitlin burst into the hall just as Ryder reached the door, grasping her arms before she came to a halt.

"Are you all right?" he demanded. "What happened?"

"Armand," she gasped. "Possessed. The walk-in…"

"He attacked you?" Ryder's voice was a low growl.

He took in her appearance in shock. Her dress was hanging from her shoulders, and he could feel the wetness of blood under his hand, see smears of red on her neck. He turned her slightly away, and his adrenaline spiked to see the ugly scratches on her pale skin, the bloodstains on the back of her gown.

Luckily the scratches were just that…shallow, only oozing blood. Even so, his own blood boiled.

"It…" she said. "It was horrible, and…it's here…."

They were surrounded now by Others, Fiona, Shauna, Jagger DeFarge.

Ryder turned to Jagger. "Bolt the doors to the outside. Don't let anyone out."

Jagger nodded and turned on his heel. Fiona and Shauna followed him, breaking into a run out of the room.

Keeping a protective arm around Caitlin, Ryder turned to the massing and muttering crowd. "Armand St. Pierre has been possessed by a walk-in. He's loose in the building."

"What does it look like?" August Gaudin demanded. "Armand or—"

"It was a creature. Huge. A cat-demon…" Caitlin struggled for words to describe it. "Part snake and bird—"

"It doesn't matter what it *looked* like," Ryder interrupted her gruffly.

Caitlin and the others turned to him, frowning— and Gaudin inhaled sharply, tense, understanding.

Ryder nodded toward them. "It's in the body of a shifter. It can look like anything now."

The assembled crowd fell silent, each looking at the others. The wave of suspicion was palpable.

Surrounded now by familiar faces, with Ryder's

protective arm around her, Caitlin managed to calm her own wild thoughts.

Beyond the immediate danger, she saw a second one: the fragile trust between the communities had only recently been restored. This new development could crumble every bridge they'd worked so hard to build.

We can't let that happen, her mind cried out. And then she felt Ryder catching her, holding her up, as her legs gave out. He lowered her to a chair.

Adrenaline crash, she realized. Ryder was on one knee in front of her, stroking her hair, and all she wanted to do was lean forward into his arms. But everyone was watching, *everyone,* and she forced herself to sit up straight, and say, "I'm fine."

"Cait, we need to know," Ryder said. He kept his voice so low that no one around them could hear. "Were there any signs St. Pierre was inhabited? Anything we can look for—anything that could be a tip-off?"

His voice was gentle, but Caitlin could feel the urgency under it, and she realized why. The entity was loose in the building, and it could look like anyone it wanted to.

She mentally kicked herself for not having noticed earlier that something was terribly, horribly wrong. *What kind of Keeper are you, that you never pick up on danger?*

"Stop it," Ryder said roughly, and Caitlin realized he had read—or understood—her thought. "None of us picked up on it. He threw this whole party, conducted this meeting, and nobody noticed a thing. It wasn't just you."

Caitlin realized with a shock that he was right. And for a moment she felt relief...and then cold fear. *How will we know?*

"Don't let on," he said softly, and stood, looking out over the crowd. His height and sense of purpose instantly caught the attention of the crowd.

"No one leaves. We split up in groups of our own kind and search the building," he announced loudly. "The Keeper will tell us what we're looking for."

Caitlin understood; it was a distraction. Keep the others busy and engaged while Jagger and the others secured the building.

"It's the voice that is most distinctive," she said, trying to keep her own voice steady. "When it speaks, you know. It sounds hollow, sibilant. It can hold a shape for a while, but when it gets...angry, excited, it slips, and the entity shows itself. Demonic. Unstable."

She raised her voice and continued while Ryder started unobtrusively for the door, following the others.

Once beyond the tall doors of the banquet hall, Ryder sprinted to catch up with Fiona, Shauna and

Jagger. "Go," he said to Jagger. "Do what you need to do. But they should stay in the hall with the others," he added, nodding his head toward the sisters.

Shauna bristled, about to protest, but Fiona held up a hand to tell her to wait as Jagger said, "Yes." And then, with a look at Fiona, he backed up, then broke into a run that turned into flight. There was a man, and then there was just the rustle of wings.

"You three sisters need to stay together." Ryder spoke to Fiona; he had no time for the youngest Keeper's temper. "Watch Caitlin."

"We will," she assured him, and took Shauna's arm.

Ryder nodded, already turning to run.

He slipped quickly through the maze of corridors and caught up with Jagger at the front door of the restaurant, where the vampire had earlier posted officers, as he had at every door.

"For all the good that will do," Ryder said grimly. "St. Pierre can take on any number of forms to get out. An insect, a spider, a mouse…"

"But you think he—it—is still here," Jagger said, and it was not a question.

"This is the second time it's directly attacked Caitlin. It wants the Keepers," Ryder said simply.

Running now, despite their long gowns, Fiona and Shauna burst into the banquet hall. The milling, chattering guests turned to look at them. August

Gaudin immediately crossed to meet them. "Where's Caitlin?" Shauna demanded.

"She just left to join you," the were said, frowning.

The hallway was deathly quiet.

As Caitlin stood in the silent corridor, she could hear her own ragged breathing…but she could see no one, no movement, in the long, dark space.

As her eyes adjusted to the dimness, lit only by faint gaslight, she was unnerved to see long gouges in the wallpaper where the demonic walk-in had leaped at her. The grooves were so deep that she suddenly realized she would have been dead if those claws had done more than graze her.

Caitlin ducked into the arched stairwell and stood with the faint, eerie Gregorian chanting all around her. She focused herself in the candlelight and slipped on a glamour. It felt even easier than usual, possibly because of the heightened adrenaline in her system. Or perhaps she, too, was feeling the effects of Samhain, when any kind of magical work was easier.

Invisible now, she moved out of the stairwell and walked carefully down the hall, her heart pounding. Even with the glamour, she knew she wasn't safe. Shapeshifters often saw through glamours, Case being a prime example, and this walk-in could even be back in the astral already, discarnate, and watching....

She approached St. Pierre's office. The door was partly open, and she halted, very still, listening....

Not a sound.

She moved to the doorway but couldn't see all the way inside, nor could she enter the office without opening the door further, announcing her presence.

She hesitated...then took a breath and entered.

She had to stifle a gasp.

The office was trashed, the furniture in splinters; it must have been the crash Caitlin had heard behind her as she fled the room. Again she marveled that she was even alive. There were more gouges by the door, long, evil-looking gashes from talons so big they could easily have severed her arm, sliced her neck open. Caitlin suppressed a shudder.

There was a sudden thump to one side of her, and she spun, startled. A candlestick rolled on the floor, near where it had fallen from a broken table.

Caitlin started to relax, then, behind her, she felt the rush of wind and whipped around....

No one in the room.

But there had been a rustling in the corridor; she was sure of it.

She moved swiftly to the door to look out.

No one in the hall...but the candles in the wall

sconces were wavering, as if someone had passed very quickly by, in a rush of air…or wings….

She could tell by the wildly fluctuating flames at the far end of the hall which direction the invisible presence had gone. She stepped out into the corridor and ran on silent feet after it.

She rounded the corner at the end of the hall and realized she was in a vestibule near the private rear entrance of the restaurant. Across the elegant parquet floor was a door she recognized as the costume room, where St. Pierre kept the finery he imposed on guests who were not attired to his satisfaction.

Caitlin quickly, quietly, crossed the floor and put her ear to the door, listening.

She heard a rustling again…like wings.

Her heart was pounding crazily, but quietly, quietly, she eased the door open….

The room was richly paneled and wallpapered, with a triple mirror on one side and dressing screens in two corners. Racks of period clothing lined the walls in tiers going all the way up to the ceiling.

Caitlin saw her own self reflected three times in the triple mirror…and a body sprawled on the floor to the side of her.

She turned quickly toward it—and gasped in shock.

Crouched over the body was the vampire Banjo Marks. He had been invisible in the mirrors.

He looked equally startled to see her, and she realized that the illusion of the glamour had vanished when she confronted herself in the mirror.

To Caitlin's horror, the gaunt and jittery vampire was brandishing a long, gleaming knife. And the body before him was recognizable by its elegant purple coat: Armand St. Pierre.

For a moment Caitlin thought the shapeshifter was dead, he was so still and pale. Then she caught the faintest sign of breath, his chest rising weakly.

"What are you doing?" she demanded of Banjo.

"It's St. Pierre. I've caught him." The vampire's features were coarsening with the onset of blood lust; his fangs were already extended and gleaming white in the dim room.

Caitlin realized she had to act quickly as he raised the knife.

"Banjo, no!" she cried out.

"This creature killed the werewolf. He nearly killed you." The vampire's eyes were red with excitement and quite probably something else.

"That was the walk-in, not Armand. Armand was possessed."

She had the strong feeling that the walk-in had left the body; Armand's crumpled form looked like the mere shell of a human being.

"I think…the walk-in is gone," she said carefully.

"I'm not taking that chance." The vampire raised the knife again.

"But it's Armand!"

She realized that on one level—on the main level—Banjo didn't care at all. In fact, the death of the shapeshifter would create a shake-up in the Council, and Banjo had had political aspirations for some time, though they'd so far gone unsatisfied, as no one trusted the unpredictable vampire. Armand St. Pierre's death would be a boon for Banjo, and that made the situation even more volatile.

She quickly calculated her options. Shapeshifters' bodies were not immortal, not in any way. They had no peculiar strengths; they were bound by the limitations of the body type and frame they had been born with. Shifting did not endow them with extra strength or powers, only the illusion of a different shape. If Banjo stabbed Armand or cut his throat, then Armand was dead; there was no mitigating the action.

Caitlin's heart was beating wildly, but she kept her voice supremely calm, even nonchalant.

"Banjo, wouldn't it be better to let the Council decide?" Quickly appealing to his political aspirations, she added, "I know it's tiresome. But you know the Council. All their rules and protocols. You know how they are about anyone from one Community disciplining someone from another."

"The interloper must die!" Banjo snarled, fangs bared.

"Agreed," Caitlin said, her voice hard. "But I have more jurisdiction than you do here. Let me do it," she said, now coaxing. "So there will be no... unpleasantness for you in the happy event that you are called to serve."

Even through whatever drugged state Banjo was in, he understood her meaning, and she could feel him wavering. She took a chance and advanced slowly, carefully, toward him.

She raised her hand just as carefully—turned it over, palm up, inviting him to give her the knife.

Outside in the hall, Ryder hovered, listening, in an agony of indecision. His instinct was to charge the room, disarm the vampire. But he could just see around the door and knew Caitlin was handling Banjo perfectly, that she might actually get the knife from him.

He had to trust her. So he waited, breath suspended....

Inside the costume room, Banjo shifted on his feet, muttering darkly, "The Council meddles where it has no business being...."

"It's intolerable," Caitlin agreed. He was just on the verge. She put her fingers lightly on his wrist. "But your time will come...."

Banjo relaxed his grip on the knife handle, and Caitlin deftly slipped the weapon from his hand.

Ryder seized the moment and burst into the room. Banjo whirled to face him, fangs elongating.

Ryder took in Armand's motionless body on the floor and followed Caitlin's lead, turning to Banjo with feigned surprise and admiration. "Excellent work—you've incapacitated him."

He saw Caitlin's eyes widen, saw that she understood.

"Banjo was brilliant," she enthused, her eyes begging Ryder to play along. "I just got here. He already had Armand completely subdued."

Hopped up as he was, Banjo was soaking up the praise. But his blood lust was still driving him. "The shifter is here now. Surely between a shifter and the Keeper of the shifters, this enemy can and should be dispatched for the sake of the Community."

Ryder knelt quickly by Armand's side and took the older shapeshifter's head in his hands, manipulating his head and neck, feigning expertise.

"It's my strong opinion that the walk-in has left this host," he announced.

Banjo's red-tinged eyes narrowed. "He could be faking," the vampire pointed out sullenly.

"True," Ryder acknowledged. "But the walk-in has had ample opportunity to overpower—" he hesitated so briefly that only Caitlin was aware that he had paused "—the Keeper, and he has not done so. I believe the entity has departed, and St. Pierre may be in need of medical assistance. We should inform the Council."

Caitlin stepped in quickly, with a cold look at Ryder. "It's Banjo's right to inform the Council." Her voice was dismissive. She turned to Banjo with feigned deference. "You were the one who overpowered him, after all."

Ryder admired her insight—enticing Banjo to leave by offering the potential of political gain.

Banjo pulled his gaunt frame up arrogantly. "I will inform the Council." He brushed past Ryder, his movements as dismissive as Caitlin's tone had been.

As soon as he was out the door, Caitlin was turning to Ryder, whispering, "Thank you."

Ryder looked down at her and also spoke quietly. Vampires were notoriously keen of hearing. "*You* did it, Caitlin. You handled him brilliantly."

Their eyes held…and then Caitlin glanced anxiously toward St. Pierre's supine body.

Ryder dropped back onto a knee beside him.

"Is he all right?" Caitlin knelt, too.

"His system has had a huge shock." Ryder used his fingers to lift Armand's eyelids. "Abnormal eye movement," he said. "Shallow breathing. And I noticed tremors before."

He took Armand's hand and dug a thumbnail into the flesh at the base of his palm. Armand didn't move.

"No response to pain," Ryder said grimly. "This looks like coma."

"Are you a doctor, too?" Caitlin asked, suddenly curious.

Ryder smiled slightly. "Hardly. But there's not always a shifter doctor around when you need one. I've picked up some skills. Do you have one?"

He meant a shifter-doctor, Caitlin knew. She felt herself bristling, indignant and proud. "Of course we do."

"Then we should get him. Or her," Ryder said. "And DeFarge, too. Armand will have to be guarded." He doubted the walk-in would return to this host, but it couldn't be ruled out.

"But Banjo—" Caitlin started, and then realized that if Banjo had actually gone straight to the Council, the room where they now stood would have been mobbed by now, Jagger, Fiona and Shauna most likely leading the pack. But the hall outside sounded empty as a tomb.

Banjo must have stopped for a little pick-me-up.

Caitlin instantly reached for her cell phone—not the easiest task, since she had put it, along with a few other essentials like lip gloss, in a garter pouch that Rosalyn had designed for costumed occasions. As she bent to raise her skirt, fumbling through yards and yards of silky gown, Ryder raised an eyebrow provocatively.

"While I would love to oblige, this hardly seems the time."

"Oh, shut up," Caitlin mumbled, reddening. She unstrapped the garter pouch and shook her skirts down, removed the cell phone and quickly started texting Fiona, Jagger and Shauna, with a 911 code in front.

Ryder stood and stepped up behind Caitlin, putting his hands on her hips as she texted, bending to put his lips close to her ear. "I would have thought you could just send a psychic message by now."

When she felt his breath in her ear, Caitlin's thumbs on the keypad slowed down as she tried to finish the text.

"I can teach you," he added, his lips brushing her earlobe. "If you're interested…"

Caitlin sent the text and pulled away from him.

"Thanks, but I *like* cell phones."

"Caitlin," Ryder said, and reached for her.

She evaded him.

"Stop it. We need a doctor. We have to…tend to Armand," she said, feeling feverish and defensive.

"I know, I—look, I'll behave."

She wavered.

He looked down for a moment at Armand's body,

and, ever mercurial, as was his tribe, there was suddenly nothing light or joking about him. "Caitlin, this isn't good. Armand is a seasoned, highly skilled shifter. For him to have been possessed like that…not to have been able to fend off the walk-in—it makes the danger so much worse than I had guessed."

Caitlin felt her heart plunging at the gravity of his tone, his words.

"And for this entity to have even attempted to possess a two-century-old Other…much less have been successful at it, and then successful in *masking* the possession…" He trailed off bleakly. "It speaks of a purpose and a focus and an ability that I don't even want to think about. It means all your Communities are in peril. Everyone."

He met her eyes and held her gaze.

Mouth dry, she spoke. "Do we tell them?"

He looked at her gravely. "This is your city. What do you think?"

She was overcome that he had asked, that he trusted her, that he was counting on her. And she knew too well from past experience that if they revealed too much, there was a big chance of causing a panic that would worsen the situation, heighten the danger and paranoia and hair-trigger reactions of the different species of Others. She started to pace as she spoke, thinking it out. "Is there any way of…feeling the entity approach? Recognizing the onslaught of possession?"

Ryder tensed, thinking, and then—as she had been afraid he would—he shook his head slowly. "They come from the astral, so there's no warning and no physical defense."

"What about a psychic defense?"

"Maybe," he said, but she could see the doubt in his face. "But if Armand was unable to defend himself, and none of us recognized the entity in him, then it was so perfectly masked that I don't know if there's any way to fend it off."

Caitlin glanced toward Armand and shivered, but she forced herself to stay focused on the problem. "You said that drugs and alcohol make humans more vulnerable to possession."

"And all kinds of psychic attack," Ryder agreed. "So all the Others need to do what they can to protect themselves psychically."

"Then that's what we need to tell them," Caitlin said. There were just as many Others who craved a high as there were humans, Case and Danny and Banjo Marks being prime examples. So at least avoiding alcohol and other mind-and-body-altering substances was something that Others could do to avoid attack. And there were also Others who practiced esoteric healing, who prayed to the gods of their choice for protection, who could summon their own spiritual strength to repel evil.

"I agree," Ryder said, and she wondered if he'd been reading her thoughts or just knew how her mind worked.

Before either of them could say anything else, there was a pounding of footsteps in the corridor, and a second later Jagger burst through the door, followed by Fiona, Shauna and the shifter-doctor, Samidha—an Indian with a Scottish-tinged accent, short, slim, butch, and frighteningly good at her job. She took one look at Armand and was instantly crossing to kneel beside him on the floor.

"The danger is that hundreds of Others will be inhabited," Jagger was saying. "Imagine the whole city overrun by Others who have been possessed. Raging entities with the powers of shifters, vampires and weres…"

Caitlin's heart began pounding wildly, charged with adrenaline at the thought of hundreds of creatures like the one that had attacked her, loose on the city.

"A massacre…" she whispered.

Chapter 19

Jagger, Fiona, Caitlin, Shauna and Ryder now stood at the head of the banquet room, in front of the assembled and restive Others. They had left Armand in Samidha's capable hands.

"It appears to be a coma," Caitlin told the Council. "Armand is alive, but his body was ravaged by the possession."

Murmurs spread throughout the crowd.

She held up a hand, and was surprised to see there was still blood on her arm from the attack of the cat demon. She pulled her eyes away from the red streaks and looked out over the crowd. "So with the death of Louis Grenville yesterday and the possession of Armand this evening, it's clear these entities, the walk-ins, are not only attacking humans but Others."

"But not vampires," Mateas Grenard said, and there was a murmur from the vampire contingent.

Jagger stepped forward sharply. "Do you know that for sure? I don't."

Grenard shifted sullenly from foot to foot. "So what are you suggesting we do?"

Now Fiona spoke. "All the Communities should be on full alert. You must spread the word to your constituencies of the danger of potentially hazardous behavior, such as drug and alcohol abuse...."

"And use your own traditions of protection to repel possession," Shauna added. "Charms, candles, rituals—use the ancient wisdom."

"It's simple. Stay off the streets and let the entities take humans instead," Mateas Grenard said loudly.

Jagger stepped forward to take control. "First things first. Tonight we go home and inform our Communities of the danger as quickly as possible. Everyone needs to know about the threat, and we need to urge our own to report any suspicious behavior, illnesses, deaths or disappearances in the last week. Then we meet again tomorrow morning, early, to share what we've learned and make a plan for tomorrow night. At Underworld," he finished, naming a jazz club owned by the vampire David Du

Lac. "At 9:00 a.m." Jagger shot a glance at David to confirm, and David nodded.

"Go, then. Go quickly," Jagger said. "And take care."

The wind snaked through the magnolia trees in the MacDonald sisters' garden, rustling the waxy leaves, casting pointillist shadows on the bricks of the courtyard below.

Inside the great room, Jagger DeFarge stood in front of the fireplace.

"You three are not going anywhere. Period," he said to the sisters.

Ryder stood against the opposite wall, radiating silent and infuriatingly male solidarity.

Jagger was immediately besieged by three angry Keepers. Fiona set the coffeepot she was holding down on the table with a crash. Shauna whirled from her restless pacing before the picture window. Caitlin jumped up from the high-backed chair where Fiona had insisted she plant herself after she'd cleaned out the scratch wounds on Caitlin's back and arms with antiseptic, antibiotic and a supercharged energetic healing powder.

And all three sisters' voices overlapped in protest.

"You can't tell us what to do, Jag, this is our *job.*"

"I think we're perfectly capable of making whatever decisions we have to make for the sake of our own Communities."

"Are you seriously trying to keep us out of this? *Seriously?*"

"Fiona," Jagger said, and to Caitlin's fury, just that was enough for Fiona to stop midsentence and hesitate, waiting. "We can't risk you. The *city* can't risk you," he said, including the other two sisters in his gaze. "Think of everything your parents worked for—died for. We can't jeopardize that."

"What makes you think *you* can handle it?" Caitlin stormed.

"Caitlin…" Fiona said.

"This is a metaphysical problem," Ryder said. "Whatever happens out there, whatever we can do on the street, that's putting a Band-Aid on the problem. What we need is a metaphysical solution. And that's your job."

"Yes," Fiona said slowly. "You're right."

Shauna frowned but said nothing.

Caitlin felt herself blazing. "You're just trying to *protect* us. We don't need protecting."

"But the city does," Jagger said.

Ryder nodded terse agreement. "We need to find the lead entity. If we cut off the head of this beast, the others will have nothing to coalesce around. But the rest of the entities will still have to be banished and *kept out* of the city, or they'll remain and continue to feed. They're mindless and will take whatever's in front of them."

"You're talking about casting a circle," Shauna said, realization in her eyes.

"A circle big enough to surround the city," Fiona finished. There was excitement in her voice—and doubt, as well.

Caitlin understood what her sisters were saying. A circle of protection could be cast around a person, a house or a building. What Ryder was suggesting was a circle to protect the entire city. It was an immense undertaking.

"The whole city…" Shauna frowned, clearly having the same misgivings as Caitlin.

"If all the Communities work together…" Fiona answered, thinking.

"It's not going to help until we get the leader," Caitlin's voice was hard. "And if it's so interested in me, then I'm the one who should be out there drawing it out."

"*No*." The other four all spoke at once.

Fiona and Jagger exchanged glances that said as clearly as if they had spoken aloud, "*I'll handle her*," and "*Thank you*."

"Caitlin, we can't do a circle without your help. It makes more sense for you to stay and work with us on that," Fiona said patiently.

"August will be here shortly, and I've already

posted several alphas at various points of the compound," Jagger said. "The sooner there's a plan for a
circle or whatever form of protection you three can
devise, the better."

"We'll be checking in regularly," Ryder said, and
without another word, the men turned and walked
out into the garden.

Caitlin turned on Fiona. "Don't you see what
they're trying to do, keeping us here? It's *our* city.
We're the Keepers. We can't just stay here, and you
can't make that decision for all of us."

She ran for the door, wincing at the sharp pain
from the scratches in her back as she twisted the
doorknob and ignoring Fiona's sharp, "Cait, no!"

The garden was windy and shadowed in the moonlight, magnolia leaves trembling, the breeze misting
water from the fountain, as Caitlin burst out the door
and followed the men across the bricks of the garden,
livid. "You can't just leave us here."

"Watch," Ryder said, without looking back at
her.

Jagger was more placating. "Caitlin, the entity has
attacked you. You've dreamed it's after you. It told
you flat out through your friend that it wants you, and
it's just as likely your sisters are in equal danger. I'm
not risking that. No one else is, either."

They had reached the front gate, and Jagger

opened it. Caitlin kept walking, fully intending to leave with them. *Just try to stop me.*

Ryder stopped in the gateway, towering over her, blocking her with his considerable frame. Caitlin dodged left, trying to get around him. He picked her up by the waist and, as she struggled in his hands, walked forward and set her down beside the fountain. With his hands still firmly around her waist, he pulled her hips forward into his and bent to kiss her, hot, slow, carnivorous. He straightened slowly, and she opened her eyes, heart racing….

And then he was gone and on the other side of the gate, a folding trick she had only seen once in her entire life.

Caitlin was momentarily stunned; then she charged the gate, but Ryder slammed it shut, whipped a key from his pocket and touched it to the lock. One of those charmed skeleton keys. Caitlin threw herself at the gate and pulled at it, but it was locked solid.

She turned and ran for the fountain, where she scrabbled along the bottom of the rim to find the hidden spare key. She hurried back to the gate and tried the key, but it wouldn't turn for anything, and the gate was as immoveable as if it had been soldered shut.

She kicked the gate, pounded on the bars…but Jagger and Ryder were long gone.

"Damn you both!" She finally leaned against the

bars of the gate, breathing hard, spent. She could feel the scratches in her back burning, blood seeping again.

How dare they? The bars of the gate only added to the feeling that she—they—were under house arrest. *Metaphysical problem my ass.*

She wasn't just furious but humiliated. It wasn't entirely true anymore that this was her responsibility, that she was the Keeper by right and duty who must oversee the repelling of this attack. All the Communities were involved now, even the vampires.

But still…

It was more her purview and charge than anyone else's, being that Ryder, their main source of information, was a shifter, the most recent victim was a shifter, and it was Danny, another shifter, through whom they had contacted the lead walk-in.

That makes it a shapeshifter case, and that makes it mine.

She felt the sudden sense of a presence, then heard a step behind her, and whirled around…to see one of the were guards who'd accompanied them home from the restaurant.

"Ms. MacDonald, let me take you inside," the young buck said, politely enough for a wolf, but there was no mistaking that this was not a request.

Caitlin narrowed her eyes. *All right, fine. I'll play along.*

She turned to the were, shrugged and smiled. "Yes, let's go."

Inside her own wing, Caitlin locked the door and breathed in deeply. She'd begged an hour for a shower and a nap, pleading exhaustion from her wounds, and although she could see Fiona's deep suspicion of her sudden compliance, she wasn't entirely faking; she *had* lost some blood, and the adrenaline crash from the attack and its aftermath was making her shaky.

Although food was the last thing on her mind, she knew some protein wouldn't hurt. After all, she had a long night ahead of her. She started for her private kitchen, then stopped.

The light-headedness she was experiencing would make an invisibility glamour that much easier to conjure. A glamour worked better on an empty stomach. And invisibility was her ticket out.

The MacDonald family had owned the compound for three generations, and over more than a century, various secret passageways had been added to the property, in case of attack. Unfortunately for Caitlin, Fiona had shared all the family secrets with Jagger, and as she slipped through the compound, masked by the glamour, she encountered a werewolf or vampire sentry at every potential escape point. If the guards had been human, Caitlin would have risked slipping by one of them, but vampires and weres had heightened senses, not to mention that extra sixth sense, that could detect her, and she didn't want to risk apprehension. She only had one shot.

Seething with frustration, she stopped in the dark courtyard to consider her options, as the wind skittered leaves across the bricks and the water whispered in the fountain.

One of the cats padded across the mossy garden stones and stopped in front of Caitlin, meowing up at her as if she could see her.

Not now, Chloe, Caitlin whispered in her head.

And then she stopped, thinking….

The young were stood dutifully but restlessly at his post in front of the garden gate. Sentry duty was an honor, but standing still was agony for a werewolf, any werewolf, much less one barely out of his teens, with all his animal hormones raging.

Then suddenly his head snapped up as he caught the soft padding of steps hurrying across the stones behind the fountain, quick and quiet, barely audible to a human but perfectly discernible to lupine ears.

The young were leaped toward the sound, loping around the fountain, snout lengthening and teeth starting to emerge in anticipation….

The were rounded the corner and stopped in his tracks.

Three pale shapes looked up at him from the garden stones—three cats.

The were looked them over in puzzlement. Was that the sound he'd heard?

While he contemplated the cats, Caitlin moved silently and invisibly past the fountain and touched her skeleton key to the gate.

The lock clicked open, the gate swung out…and she was gone.

Chapter 20

Caitlin walked through the raucous neon carnival of Bourbon Street, cloaked in her glamour. On some level she knew without a doubt it was a stupid thing to do, an impulsive act prompted by anger, spite, resentment, payback…and that nagging feeling of inadequacy that never left her, the need to prove herself, to be worthy of her position, her charge, her family, her city.

But also, she could not help thinking, could not *stop* thinking, that Ryder and Jagger were simply wrong. It would do no earthly good for them to go out on the streets looking for these creatures, these entities. There were only two occasions when any of them had been in direct contact with the lead walk-in: in the séance with Danny, and when Armand had talked to her, just before attacking her.

And the séance was the only time they had been able to actually *summon* the thing. Danny had known exactly how—and where—to go, and he had done it within minutes.

So it only made sense that if they were to catch the lead entity, what they needed was not an army of Others patrolling the streets or encircling the city with a magic spell. What they needed was Danny.

And that was her plan. She would get Danny, bring him back to the compound, and they would summon the entity through him, with him. Ryder could finish the ritual that had been interrupted the night of the séance, and once the thing had been cast into outer darkness, they could work on protecting the rest of the city.

Simple.

Bourbon was packed, of course, this being the night before Halloween, so many people in costume that the date seemed to be a technicality. But Caitlin knew that whatever looked like excess now would be exponentially excessive by tomorrow night.

There was already a Halloween feeling hanging over the street, though, and Caitlin didn't like it. She preferred to celebrate Samhain with quiet, restorative rituals in the woods, cloaked in soft night, under the pure moon, to celebrate god and goddess and the earth with dancing, blessings, healing charms. A far cry from the throngs screaming to be heard over "Psycho Killer" and "Werewolves of London" and "The Monster Mash" and "Thriller," all blasting from the open doors and windows of various clubs.

Although she could see some charming, playful costumes—fairies, Harry Potter characters, silver-screen stars—there were far too many that Caitlin found disturbing: serial killers from slasher movies, "victims" with fake hatchets seemingly buried in their heads. Zombies were particularly prevalent this year, some cultural trend that Caitlin was unable to wrap her mind around.

Why people had to concentrate on the negative on this night, she'd never been able to understand. On a pagan holy day, especially the equinoxes and solstices, there was such a power for magnification and manifestation. Who in their right mind would want to manifest an ax in the head?

And perhaps she was simply still shaken from the demon attack, but tonight Bourbon, with its ca-cophony of music and kaleidoscope of lights, seemed to take all the ugliness of Halloween and magnify it—the flaming jack-o'-lanterns, the spiders, the serial killers. And of course, there was the alcohol. Always the alcohol, and there were other substances, other highs, in evidence here, as well—revelers so stoned their eyes were dead as they stumbled past like the zombies some of them were dressed as. Every drunk tourist seemed malevolent. Exactly the circumstances Ryder had been talking about, the danger...

The crowd had become so thick that Caitlin's feet had slowed almost to a standstill; the intersection was swarmed with people in all four directions, and no one was moving. So far it had not been an issue to brush against people on the crowded streets; no one had freaked at coming into contact with an essentially invisible person, because there were so many other people about that any time Caitlin had accidentally bumped into a passerby, there was always someone else—someone visible—right beside her who could have made the contact.

But now she was surrounded so closely that she was being pressed on all sides. And the pressure was only getting stronger, as the crowd was surging forward in all directions, a crushing rush...and there were so many tall people around her that she was no longer able even to see anything. And more than that, there was a feeling, an ominous feeling, of threat.

Feeling desperate, Caitlin swiveled her head... and with a dawning horror realized that every person around her was menacing...every one with disturbing eyes...the black, malevolent eyes she had seen in Danny during the séance, and in Armand just before he shifted into the cat demon. And they were all staring at her. They could *see* her—even through her glamour.

These revelers were not fake zombies. They were the real thing. Possessed.

As Caitlin opened her mouth to scream, a cloak was thrown over her head and pulled tight around her face. Darkness descended, and strong, cruel arms grabbed her around the waist and shoulders, and shuffled her forward.

No one heard her scream over the clashing layers of music.

The cluster of zombies moved in a solid group, with Caitlin pinioned between arms and legs and torsos in the center, barreling forward and driving through the crowd in front of them, which parted slowly, like a sluggish wave, and before Caitlin could think, they had swept her into what she somehow sensed was an alley and through a waiting open door.

"She'll never stay put," Ryder worried aloud as vampire and shapeshifter strode, tall and long-legged, through the crowds on Bourbon, toward Bons Temps. The people were packed wall-to-wall—it was only the combined intimidating presence and grim looks of purpose of the two men that cleared them a path through the costumed revelers.

"Don't worry about Caitlin. She's a handful, but Fiona will take care of her," Jagger assured him.

"I don't doubt Fiona can handle just about anything," Ryder answered. *Everything except her sister. I can't even handle her sister.*

The tight feeling in his stomach intensified. He stared out over the crowds before them. "It might as well be Halloween," he said aloud. A human would not have been able to hear him in the raucous crowd, but a vampire could literally hear a pin drop, even with a din like this.

A muscle jumped in Jagger's jawline, and though he said nothing, Ryder knew the vampire had the same fear he did: that there was no guarantee the entities would wait until the next evening to descend on the street.

Ryder tried to focus on the plan. They were headed toward Bons Temps. Much as Ryder hated to admit it, the only solid connection they had to the lead walk-in was Caitlin's druggie psychic shapeshifter friend, Danny. He hadn't wanted to tell Caitlin, but it was clear that their best bet to trap and bind the lead entity, to perform the exorcism that he had been unable to complete the night of the séance, was to convince the young psychic to do another sitting.

Caitlin might have been the best person to do that, but Ryder thought that, shifter to shifter, he might just be able to *make* it happen. Especially if he mentioned that Caitlin had been attacked again.

The thought made his blood rise.

He knew she was furious with him for leaving her. But he would risk her wrath to keep her safe. He would be damned if he would lose someone else…

*Someone else I love…*to the walk-ins.

Love. Yes, he really had thought that. Really did feel it.

He would do whatever he had to do to protect Caitlin MacDonald. And her sisters, too.

Inside—*a warehouse?*—was worse than outside. Heavy doors clanged shut, and there was a sudden, crashing silence, broken only by the inhuman shuffling and labored breathing of her captors, who held her with a mass of arms and hands.

Hooded, blinded, Caitlin ordered her screaming nerves to still and forced herself to take notice of her surroundings. Caitlin could smell must and mold, which, since Katrina, had lingered pervasively in almost every building in the Quarter. There was a wetness to the air, as well.

She could hear only faintly through the thick wool cloak that encompassed her, but the sounds seemed echoey, as if they were in a very large room, a high-ceilinged room. They didn't seem to shift direction to avoid any furniture as the cluster of zombies shuffled her on. She was as stiff-legged as they were, frozen into the sheer numbness of terror.

There was a creaking that could only be a door opening, and a rush of air that she could feel on her calves, the only part of her body not covered by the cloak. She was jostled through into another room—even in her terror, she recognized the sensation of crossing a threshold, the opening feeling that moving through a doorway evoked. And it was a large one, too, tall double doors, she thought.

There was something instantly different about the atmosphere here; still the mustiness, the dampness, but mixed with a different smell entirely. Sweat and sulfur…ammonia…

And there were other people in the room, too. The hairs on Caitlin's arms lifted as she realized… there were not just other people in the room but *many* others. She could hear breathing, feel their presence, but there were no words, no sounds but their breath.

Dead? Zombies?

No. Drugged. The bite of ammonia—it was the acrid smell of crack.

Her captors inched forward, then stopped, and Caitlin could feel some of them step away, as if they had reached their destination. She felt adrenaline spike through her veins.

Someone pulled the cloak off her, and she gasped in air, blinking quickly to force her eyes to adjust to the darkness around her.

It was dim, windowless except for a few narrow slits high above, a huge warehouse space with unfinished walls, intricate systems of pipes and beams high above, and obvious mold stains on the wood. A shell of a building that had been rotting since Katrina. Hazy smoke floated in the air, and she realized why she had been feeling the presence of so many bodies. This was a crack house. The half-present feeling came from unconsciousness.

Caitlin stared around her through the hypnotic drifting smoke, her nostrils burning from the stinging smell of crack, and felt a surge of horror at being surrounded by addicts. She had a sudden flash of insight: the Others might not be human, but these street junkies were truly the undead.

A figure stepped out of the darkness, moving sinuously toward her. The other creatures shuffled around her in a mindless kind of anticipation, and Caitlin went light-headed with fear. She instinctively stepped backward…and felt the pressure of a body behind hers, several bodies, the circle of mindless souls who had brought her into this pit. Then the dim light from the few high windows illuminated the face of the figure standing before her and the features were so familiar that Caitlin had a wave of mind-numbing relief: Danny. That pale, young skin, shimmering dark hair…and those bottomless eyes.

Caitlin's relief dissolved into terror as Danny smiled, a smile that didn't reach his eyes and that was not his own.

The voice that hissed through his mouth confirmed her worst fear.

It was the voice of the walk-in.

"Welcome, Keeper."

Ryder and Jagger were crossing Toulouse Street, approaching Bons Temps, when Ryder felt a scream.

He froze midstride.

Jagger looked at him sharply. "What?"

"There was…a scream…."

Jagger looked understandably perplexed. This was Bourbon Street on a Friday night. People were screaming all around them, screaming to make themselves heard, screaming along with the music, or just screaming to scream.

"In the astral," Ryder said, and his heart contracted in pain and terror. "It's Cait."

"Tell me what you want me to do," Jagger said instantly, and meant it.

Ryder forced himself to breathe, to focus through his concern. "Call the Keepers. Get back to them. See if they have any idea where she's gone."

"She may be there, you know—" Jagger began, an attempt at reassurance.

"She's not," Ryder cut him off, and the vampire didn't even try to protest further but lifted his iPhone.

"Go back to them. If there's anything they can do, do it, but keep them safe," Ryder told him.

"What will you do?" Jagger paused, the phone still in his hand.

"Find her shapeshifter friends. Find *her*," Ryder said, and he shifted into his subtle body and then was gone in a rush of black wings.

Chapter 21

The volume inside Bons Temps was approaching apocalyptic as Ryder touched down on the sidewalk in the bird's body and instantly shifted back to himself. He strode in off the street and muscled his way through the pressed-together, sweating, undulating patrons. He scanned the stage. The band was a ragtag combination of musicians, typical Bourbon Street, hard partiers with impressive music skills.

The long-haired psychic, Danny, was not on stage, but the front man was instantly recognizable. The anorexic musician's build and cocky swagger would have been a good hint, but the subtly shifting facial features were a dead giveaway. Case. Even in his state of high anxiety and focus, Ryder had to admire the kid's control. It took a lot of skill to hold a partial shift like that just on its own, much less while performing, and no doubt high on something—there was something just a bit too manic about his frenzied performance.

Even so, Case lasered in on him, noticing him in the crowd, electric-blue eyes sizzling from the stage, measuring, calculating.

Ryder used the connection to project an intent, not a request, but a demand. He saw Case receive it, flinch back slightly, and then those eyes went icy, antagonistic. For a moment Ryder thought he might have gone too far, but then there was a flickering, a shift in the current vibrating between them, and the jolt of antagonism lessened. Somehow the younger man had gotten a deeper message: the urgency of Ryder's presence.

Ryder held Case's eyes, then turned and moved through the crowd toward the back courtyard.

The night was dark and humid, misty with a diffuse haze that blurred the neon lights of the bar signs, creating an altered-world space appropriate to the occasion.

Ryder paced the slate stones of the courtyard, unable to keep still. In all likelihood Caitlin had been gone for more than an hour, since the moment he and Jagger had left the sisters' compound. He cursed himself for his stupidity; how could he not have known this about her by now? He could have chained her, and she would have found a way to follow. He only prayed that he would have the opportunity *not* to make the same mistake again.

In truth, as a creature of the nineteenth century, he had not caught up to the vastness of change in the feminine consciousness. They were equals now. He was a fool not to have absorbed that.

He had wounded Caitlin's sense of duty, her feminine pride, and she had reacted in a completely predictable way that meant he could lose her forever. The city could lose her forever. The world could lose her forever. An irredeemable loss.

There was no sound behind him, but he sensed a disturbance in the astral, the presence of another shifter. He turned sharply.

Case stood in the passageway from the back door to the courtyard, slouch-hipped, arrogant.

The two men stared at each other through the dark; then Case sauntered forward, all Louisiana cool, removing a joint and lighter from an inside pocket and firing up the lighter. As he started to raise the flame, Ryder stepped forward with one long stride and plucked the joint from his lips, tossed it aside.

Case's face rippled with rage.

"What the—" the younger man began in a fury.

Ryder held up a hand. "Cait's in trouble," he said, cutting Case off.

The musician's face didn't change, but Ryder felt the disturbance in his subtle body; it was hard not to.

"Ask me, she was in trouble the minute she met you, Ace." Case pulled out a pack of Marlboros and removed one, lit up. Ryder winced at the thought of all that potential, swirling down the toilet of addiction.

It was hard not to think of himself at that age.

But all of that was a diversion so that he could not, for a moment, think about what Case had just said. Which he knew in his heart to be true.

Ryder tried to center himself, to breathe. "She's disappeared," he said as calmly as he could manage. "My guess is she's gone to find your mutual friend."

"And?" Case said maddeningly.

Ryder held his temper. "It's very dangerous for her out there right now. Dangerous for anyone, but especially for her and her sisters."

"And this has *what* to do with me?"

"Don't bullshit me. You care for her. I know you do." Ryder stared straight into Case's eyes. "Regardless of how you hurt her, you care."

"Who's bullshitting who, shifter?" Case smiled, a crazy cracked watermelon grin that didn't quite make it to his eyes. "How *I* hurt her is nothing compared to what damage *you're* about to do. At least I never pretended to be anything but what I am. I never promised anything, in word or deed. Can you say the same thing?"

Ryder was struck dumb by the young shifter's insight.

"Right—tell me you didn't promise *everything*, even if you never said a word." Case waited until he saw that the whole truth had sunk deep into Ryder's bones, and then he dragged on his cigarette and exhaled, shrugging.

"But don't feel too bad about it. It's our nature, after all, isn't it? And who knows that better than sweet Cait?"

Ryder felt sick with the truth of it.

Case's face hardened. "Well, maybe she went out there in that crazy little way she has—because she doesn't care what happens to her. She knows you'll be gone on the next train, or tradewind. I know Sister Goldenhair. She'll go out fighting, save everyone she can in the battle—but when her light goes out…"

He removed the cigarette from his mouth and let it fall to the slate flooring to explode in glowing ash, then crushed the butt out.

"So no," he said softly. "Don't you be guilt-tripping me. I'm the small sin here, shifter. The lesser of two evils."

Ryder reached out and grabbed the lapels of Case's

leather jacket, and in that moment, he could have ripped the other man to shreds. But he forced himself to breathe, to steady.

"So we've both done her dirt. Are you going to do something about it? Because *I* am."

He felt Case's fury, and suddenly he was holding nothing. The young shifter was standing several feet back from him. He'd folded, very skillfully. From the new distance, he stared at Ryder stonily. "Difference between you and me, Ace, is I don't pretend to be a hero."

"Cait doesn't need a hero. She needs help."

"Might as well let her go. You'll only end up hurting her, because you can never settle for just one life—or girl. That's a shifter's nature, and you know it just as well as I do. You're already looking toward the new city, the new body. It's our nature to shift... shifter."

Ryder summoned every ounce of control he had. "Play the cynic all you want, but I know the truth about *you*, too. You may be a shifter and a junkie, but you're capable of loyalty toward your friends. Cait's in danger, and your pal Danny, too, and I think you're coming with me."

Case stared at him for such a long moment Ryder thought he'd lost, and then the young shifter spoke.

"That would imply you knew where to find them, and we both know you don't."

Ryder said, "No. But you do."

Chapter 22

Caitlin stared at Danny-not-Danny through the haze of crack smoke in the warehouse. There was something so alien about him that it chilled her—the sinuous way he moved as he slowly circled her, as if there were actually something else inside him using his body in a completely different way, not human, not shifter, but Else.

As if reading her thoughts, the walk-in smiled, and that was an abomination, too. There was the telltale sibilance in its consonants as it spoke. "Yes. I am pleased with this body. Its powers are more subtle than the older one...."

Caitlin thought fleetingly that it must have meant Armand.

"And it knows how to procure its pleasures, this host. I approve." The creature's glittering eyes swept over Caitlin's body, and she suddenly felt naked, exposed. "But time for a new one now, I think."

Caitlin's blood froze, and for a moment, as she envisioned a horrible half-supernatural rape, her mind went black with terror. But then, through the choking nausea of the thought, she realized that the creature wanted something far more lethal than an invasion of her body. It wanted full possession of her.

Her mind raced through the scenario. If the walk-in had been able to mimic Armand so that not even his own employees or fellow shifters recognized the possession, then the walk-in would be able to use her own body to gain entry to the compound, to walk right into Fiona's rooms, into Shauna's....

She shuddered with fear and rage—and then a cold determination that she would die before letting that happen.

The creature must have felt the change in her, because Danny's body shifted, rippled, so that for a moment there was something demonic there, skeletal and rotting, that had only the slightest hint of Danny's humanity. She could even smell it, a stench like a rotting corpse.

"Yes," it said sibilantly. "Take the Keepers, then take the city."

No, she thought violently. *I'll die first.*

Danny's face tightened in rage. "Hold her!" the walk-in screamed. Two of the zombified tourists moved faster than the others, shockingly fast, and seized Caitlin by the arms.

Then one said, low and rough in her ear, "Fight. Keep moving."

The familiar voice sent a surge of shock and relief through her body. *Ryder.* She obeyed instantly and began to struggle with her captors with all her might.

"Seize her! Hold her!" the walk-in shrieked.

The men holding her were moving in tandem, shoving her between them, but not with an intent to injure, just to create a moving blur of bodies.

Suddenly Caitlin felt the shimmering, the wave of heat that accompanied a shift, but stronger than she had ever felt it, coming from all sides, enveloping her, and she gasped aloud to see herself in the hands of—*herself.* Twice. Ryder and Case had taken on her own form. The sight was so startling that she almost forgot Ryder's directive to keep moving. She had seen herself in mirrors thousands of times, but this was a completely different experience, like meeting herself in a dream, a familiar face and body, but as a stranger. She saw herself fully for the very first time:

beautiful, vulnerable, fierce, loving, wanting…things she had never seen in herself before. And powerful. Unbelievably powerful. For a moment she could do nothing but stare.

A split second later she realized the plan. There were three of her now, and the walk-ins wouldn't know which of her to grab.

The thing that was in Danny was prowling, still shrieking, "Seize her!" But the shuffling creatures around them were swaying in their tracks, muttering, confused.

The three Caitlins ceased their merry-go-round scramble and stood with backs to each other, facing outward.

"What now?" Case as Caitlin whispered harshly.

"We incapacitate the leader," Ryder as Caitlin whispered back.

"Don't hurt him," Caitlin begged, alarmed for Danny.

"We bind the entity. Follow my lead," Ryder said.

Caitlin felt Ryder link his arm through hers and automatically did the same with Case on her other side. She saw Case joining arms with Ryder, forming a living triangle.

And then Ryder called out in Caitlin's own voice, "*Quod perditum est, invenietur. Te implor, Doamne, nu ignora aceasta rugaminte. Nici mort,*

*nici al fiintei... Lasa orbita sa fie vasul care-i va
transporta, sufletul la el. Asa sa fie! Asa sa fie!
Acum! Acum!*"

Caitlin followed the words in her head.

*I command you, unclean spirit, whoever you are,
to hear and obey me to the letter, I who am a minister
of the light despite my unworthiness. You shall not be
emboldened to harm in any way this creature of light,
or these bystanders. You are bound by my words.*

Caitlin was astonished at the power in Ryder—and
by the fact that it was her own self she was seeing,
some powerful, unshakable blend of the two of them.
His whole body was straining next to hers, taut and
filled with the conviction of his words.

"I cast you out, unclean spirit, along with every
power of darkness, every spectre from hell, and all
your fell companions. Begone and stay far from this
creature of light. Hearken, therefore, and tremble in
fear, you foe of all living races, you begetter of death,
you robber of life, you corrupter of justice, you root
of all evil."

Around the three of them, the mass of zombielike
possessed were swaying and muttering incoherently,
disturbed and disturbing. The walk-in itself undulated
in Danny's body, a horrible sight, as if a mass of
snakes was moving under his skin.

Ryder continued the ritual, relentless.

"You are guilty before the whole human race, and

all the races of Others, to whom you proffered by your enticements the poisoned cup of death. Depart, then, transgressor. Depart, seducer, full of lies and cunning, foe of virtue, persecutor of the innocent. Give place, abominable creature, give way, you monster, give way. We cast you forth into the outer darkness, where everlasting ruin awaits you and your abettors. We cast you forth into outer darkness. We cast you forth into outer darkness."

The Caitlin who was Ryder glanced to the other two, and Caitlin realized with a jolt what the look meant. She lifted her voice and chanted with Ryder, and heard Case on the other side of her chanting with them.

"We cast you forth into outer darkness. We cast you forth into outer darkness. We cast you forth into outer darkness…."

Danny's face rippled as the walk-in struggled to maintain control of the body. It whiplashed, snapping back and forth like a green sapling in a hurricane-force wind. And then it forced itself upright, and with a savage cry, it clenched its fists and raised them up in triumph.

"Still here, bounty hunter. Still here!" It gloated and capered. And all the zombified tourists shuffled and gibbered around it, catching the frenzy….

Caitlin felt a rush of anger—and fear. *It's winning. We can't do this. It's too strong.*

And then she realized what was missing. It was so obvious. "Danny, you have to help us," she cried out.

Case stiffened beside her, understanding instantly. "Danny, wake up in there. We need you. Push that bastard out."

Beside them, Ryder never stopped chanting, and now Caitlin and Case joined him again, chanting with all the force in their bodies. "We cast you forth into outer darkness. We cast you forth into outer darkness. We cast you forth into outer darkness...."

The walk-in suddenly shuddered as if struck by lightning from within. Its body twisted, arched, and it threw back its head and howled in rage, a rage that reverberated in the vast warehouse space, a more than human sound, growing, shaking the burned walls.

And then the howl evaporated, diminishing, fading, as if sucked into some other dimension.

And Danny's body crumpled in front of them, like a marionette whose strings had been cut.

Instantly the others shuffling around them stopped their frenzied movement, one by one crumpling leglessly to the cement floor.

The three Caitlins stood in the middle of the floor, with inert bodies all around them. The warehouse looked like a tableau of a battleground, frozen in time....

Then two of the Caitlins shimmered, shifted,

with that nauseating ripple of reality…and Ryder and Case stood in front of her, the three of them dazed, shocked, grateful.

And then Danny's crumpled body stirred ever so slightly on the floor, and while Case leaped forward to crouch by his friend's side, Ryder seized Caitlin and held her, held her as if he would never let her go.

Chapter 23

As is eternally true, it took the whole Community to set a great evil right.

On Samhain's Eve, on the banks of the Mississippi in Algiers, centuries-old meeting place for conjuring, they gathered, all the Communities, and stood together in a clearing by their great river, under the moon, circles within circles, vampires, werewolves, shapeshifters and Keepers…to push. They pushed with all the powers they had as species, and with all the power of love for their families and fellows… pushed at the evil that had descended on their city, pushed at the formless entities, pushed them onto the wind that rode their mighty river. And the entities were swept away by the invisible broom of love and protection, and the wind took them and carried them, carried them along the inexorable river, carried them out to disperse over the sea.

And when the wind had taken them, the Others took a collective breath, and, summoning all their most cherished traditions and wisdom and power, they set a protective barrier around the city, layers of protection from each of their traditions, all woven into a psychic web that would repel any attack for months to come, long enough for the walk-ins to scatter and move far, far beyond the sphere of New Orleans. Their leader had been banished to outer darkness. They would not mass again.

The force of the ritual was so powerful that the Halloween revelers on Bourbon Street paused in their debauchery, wondering why they suddenly felt... lighter. A few even pushed away from the bar and turned to dance with their companions instead.

And after the Communities had stood quietly in the moonlight, feeling the power of the magic they had done, they began a celebration of their own, where every Other was welcome and loved for whoever, whatever, they were, and the wine flowed, and shrimp and crawfish boiled, and gumbo and jambalaya steamed.

Ryder had seen Case among the shapeshifters during the ritual; Danny was recovering, but still too weak to leave his bed.

Ryder had been surprised to see the cocky young shifter hovering uncomfortably at the periphery of the partying crowd, chain-smoking like a chimney, looking ready to bolt at any second.

Before he could, Ryder circled around to him, stopped a casual distance away and lifted his Abita bottle in greeting. "That ought to hold the suckers for a while," he said casually.

For a moment Case looked startled—startled to be noticed, startled to be addressed, startled that it was Ryder speaking to him. He nodded, warily.

Ryder took a swig of his beer, looked off across the river at the lights of the Crescent City.

"Of course, magic never holds them off for long. There's always something out there…waiting. We can never let our guard down."

"We," Case said, without inflection, but his scorn dripped from the words nonetheless.

Ryder said nothing. The moon shimmered off the river.

The young shapeshifter dragged on his cigarette. "You plannin' on sticking around, Ace? That's a new one."

"I'd forgotten how much there is to love about this city."

"The city," Case repeated contemptuously.

"Everything about her," Ryder said, and didn't try to hide what he meant.

"Yeah," Case said.

"You can do better than this," Ryder said abruptly.

Case glanced at him sideways. "Better than what?"

"Better than everything. You have talent, and I'm not just talking about music. You have the kind of talent almost no one else has. Why waste it? Talent is a gift—it's not to be taken lightly, or squandered." Ryder felt a ripple of déjà vu about the words he had just spoken. It was the same conversation he had had with his own mentor.

The arrogant young shapeshifter standing before him was downright hostile…just as he himself had been, all those years ago.

"You deal with yours, I'll deal with mine," Case sneered.

"Even if it kills you, huh?"

"My business, Ace," Case flung over his shoulder as he flicked his cigarette aside and started away.

"Why not try something different? You *and* your friend?" Ryder said, and he saw Case falter at the last words. Ryder moved a scant step closer across the dewy grass and spoke softly. "He keeps going like this, he's dead in six months, three months…. You know it."

Case didn't move, but Ryder felt a ripple in the subtle body of the younger man.

"Give me six weeks. I can show you what my teacher showed me. You don't like it—what's the harm?"

Case turned on his boot heel, staring at Ryder murderously. "You out to save my soul, shifter?" he mocked.

"Maybe save your ass. Your soul is up to you."

The two men regarded each other for a long, un-compromising moment.

"I'll think about it," Case said.

Ryder nodded.

And then Case tipped a hand to his head, mock-ingly, did a little spin and was gone.

Ryder looked into the dark where he had disap-peared and felt himself smile. The kid had no idea he was about to be hung upside down in a tree for nine days and nine nights. Enlightenment came at a cost. But if nothing else, it would stop the smoking.

Caitlin sat at the long table by the river, the one set up for the Keepers. Fiona and Shauna were out dancing on the scraggly grass to the sexy musical drawl of the Zydeco band. She saw them in the crowd, giddy, laughing, sparkling…and she recognized the feeling; it was the endorphin rush of a spell well-cast, of magic that had found its mark and achieved its highest, purest purpose.

They had triumphed this time. The city was safe, her sisters were safe, and there was a new bond among the Others—the whole underworld had united in peace and strength, and if they could all just keep this feeling, Caitlin knew that there was a whole new era of community and cooperation ahead.

So why did she feel like crying?

She was missing their parents, it was true. The ancient meeting place of Algiers always gave her that pang.

But if she were honest, truly honest, with herself, she was missing more than their parents.

The job was done. And that meant Ryder was done, too.

She'd known all along, of course, and she'd done everything in her power to keep him at bay, knowing this day would come, knowing that he would do what shifters do best: shift. Change. Move. Leave her.

She felt herself tremble, dangerously close to tears, and she forced the feeling away angrily.

She had her city. She had her work. She had her family. She didn't need him. She would survive.

Someone stepped up behind her, a looming presence that made her tense instinctively, nerves still jumping....

And then Ryder put a foot over the bench of the picnic table and sat beside her, facing her, his legs open, thighs brushing hers.

If it were possible to freeze and melt at the same

time, Caitlin did in that moment—her face flaming and her heart crying and her body stiffening to statuelike rigidity all at the same time.

Ryder looked into her face, full on, his green eyes steady on hers. "You did it, Keeper," he said, without a trace of mockery. "I knew you were good, that first day in the shop."

Caitlin used all the force of will she possessed to answer lightly. "You didn't seem all that sure, actually."

"Then I was wrong," he said, holding her gaze.

For a moment she felt herself lost, drowning; then she looked away. "When do you go?"

She couldn't look at him, so she focused on the river, the moon—and breathing. He didn't answer… and didn't answer, and she found suddenly she wasn't breathing anymore.

"Caitlin," he said. She felt his fingers close around her hand, and she had to turn her head to look at him. He was like a Greek god in the moonlight, so beautiful to her that she couldn't speak.

"Cait, I want to stay, if you'll have me."

Caitlin felt fire through her chest, a hot ache that made tears spring to her eyes. She couldn't make herself believe what she was hearing.

Ryder reached out, took her face gently in both huge hands—so, so gentle and strong—and his fingers moved on her cheeks, brushing away her tears. "Will you?"

And then she was crying, as he pulled her to him… and she was home.

* * * * *

COMING NEXT MONTH

Available November 30, 2010

HARLEQUIN®

A Romance

FOR EVERY MOOD™

Spotlight on

Classic

Quintessential, modern love stories
that are romance at its finest.

See the next page
to enjoy a sneak peek from
the Harlequin® Romance series.

*See below for a sneak peek from our classic
Harlequin® Romance® line.*

Introducing DADDY BY CHRISTMAS by Patricia Thayer.

MIA caught sight of Jarrett when he walked into the open lobby. It was hard not to notice the man. In a charcoal business suit with a crisp white shirt and striped tie covered by a dark trench coat, he looked more Wall Street than small-town Colorado.

Mia couldn't blame him for keeping his distance. He was probably tired of taking care of her.

Besides, why would a man like Jarrett McKane be interested in her? Why would he want to take on a woman expecting a baby? Yet he'd done so many things for her. He'd been there when she'd needed him most. How could she not care about a man like that?

Heart pounding in her ears, she walked up behind him. Jarrett turned to face her. "Did you get enough sleep last night?"

"Yes, thanks to you," she said, wondering if he'd thought about their kiss. Her gaze went to his mouth, then she quickly glanced away. "And thank you for not bringing up my meltdown."

Jarrett couldn't stop looking at Mia. Blue was definitely her color, bringing out the richness of her eyes.

"What meltdown?" he said, trying hard to focus on what she was saying. "You were just exhausted from lack of sleep and worried about your baby."

He couldn't help remembering how, during the night, he'd kept going in to watch her sleep. How strange was that? "I hope you got enough rest."

She nodded. "Plenty. And you're a good neighbor for

coming to my rescue."

He tensed. Neighbor? *What neighbor kisses you like I did?* "That's me, just the full-service landlord," he said, trying to keep the sarcasm out of his voice. He started to leave, but she put her hand on his arm.

"Jarrett, what I meant was you went beyond helping me." Her eyes searched his face. "I've asked far too much of you."

"Did you hear me complain?"

She shook her head. "You should. I feel like I've taken advantage."

"Like I said, I haven't minded."

"And I'm grateful for everything…"

Grasping her hand on his arm, Jarrett leaned forward. The memory of last night's kiss had him aching for another. "I didn't do it for your gratitude, Mia."

Gorgeous tycoon Jarrett McKane has never believed in Christmas—but he can't help being drawn to soon-to-be-mom Mia Saunders! Christmases past were spent alone…and now Jarrett may just have a fairy-tale ending for all his Christmases future!

*Available December 2010,
only from Harlequin® Romance®.*

REQUEST YOUR
FREE BOOKS!
2 FREE NOVELS PLUS 2 FREE GIFTS!

nocturne™

Dramatic and Sensual Tales of Paranormal Romance.

YES! Please send me 2 FREE Harlequin® Nocturne™ novels and my 2 FREE gifts (gifts are worth about $10). After receiving them, if I don't wish to receive any more books, I can return the shipping statement marked "cancel." If I don't cancel, I will receive 4 brand-new novels every other month and be billed just $4.47 per book in the U.S. or $4.99 per book in Canada. That's a saving of at least 15% off the cover price! It's quite a bargain! Shipping and handling is just 50¢ per book.* I understand that accepting the 2 free books and gifts places me under no obligation to buy anything. I can always return a shipment and cancel at any time. Even if I never buy another book from Harlequin, the two free books and gifts are mine to keep forever.

238/338 HDN E9M2

Name   (PLEASE PRINT)

Address   Apt. #

City   State/Prov.   Zip/Postal Code

Signature (if under 18, a parent or guardian must sign)

Mail to the **Reader Service:**
IN U.S.A.: P.O. Box 1867, Buffalo, NY 14240-1867
IN CANADA: P.O. Box 609, Fort Erie, Ontario L2A 5X3

Not valid for current subscribers to Harlequin Nocturne books.

Want to try two free books from another line?
Call 1-800-873-8635 or visit www.ReaderService.com.

* Terms and prices subject to change without notice. Prices do not include applicable taxes. N.Y. residents add applicable sales tax. Canadian residents will be charged applicable provincial taxes and GST. Offer not valid in Quebec. This offer is limited to one order per household. All orders subject to approval. Credit or debit balances in a customer's account(s) may be offset by any other outstanding balance owed by or to the customer. Please allow 4 to 6 weeks for delivery. Offer available while quantities last.

Your Privacy: Harlequin Books is committed to protecting your privacy. Our Privacy Policy is available online at www.ReaderService.com or upon request from the Reader Service. From time to time we make our lists of customers available to reputable third parties who may have a product or service of interest to you. If you would prefer we not share your name and address, please check here. ☐

Help us get it right—We strive for accurate, respectful and relevant communications. To clarify or modify your communication preferences, visit us at www.ReaderService.com/consumerschoice.

HN10

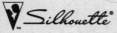

ROMANTIC

SUSPENSE

Sparked by Danger, Fueled by Passion.

RACHEL LEE

A Soldier's Redemption

When the Witness Protection Program fails at keeping Cory Farland out of harm's way, ex-marine Wade Kendrick steps in. As Cory's new bodyguard, Wade has a plan for protecting her—however falling in love was not part of his plan.

Available in December wherever books are sold.

Visit Silhouette Books at www.eHarlequin.com

SRS27705

Silhouette® *Desire*

USA TODAY bestselling authors

MAUREEN CHILD

and

SANDRA HYATT

UNDER THE MILLIONAIRE'S MISTLETOE

Just when these leading men thought they had it all figured out, they quickly learn their hearts have made other plans. Two passionate stories about love, longing and the infinite possibilities of kissing under the mistletoe.

Available December
wherever you buy books.

Always Powerful, Passionate and Provocative.

SD73069